THE CIRCUS LIGHTS

THE SLIM HARDY MYSTERIES #8

JACK BENTON

ALSO BY JACK BENTON

The Slim Hardy Mystery Series

The Tokyo Lost Series

For Miffy
much more than just a cat

THE CIRCUS LIGHTS

1

IT WAS A STUPID IDEA, JOHN "SLIM" Hardy thought as he stood by the window—the darkness outside providing a reflection in the absence of an actual mirror—and adjusted the collar on the black shirt he had hastily bought that afternoon out of the clothing section of his local supermarket. He had conveniently had a haircut just a couple of days earlier and had trimmed his greying beard. In his only decent pair of jeans he looked borderline respectable. Then, with a sudden engine roar, the lights of a car flickered across the window of his downstairs flat, momentarily erasing the reflection as though he were nothing more than a ghost, and Slim considered bailing on the whole thing.

He might well have done, but he had forgotten to charge his phone, and by the time he located his charger, he had come back around to the idea. As he checked his wallet for money and pulled on his coat, he gave a wry shake of his head.

It didn't seem right.

Slim Hardy didn't go on blind dates.

Yet here he was, heading out of the door. He wondered as he turned the Yale lock whether he ought to put on some aftershave, but thought that might be pushing it a bit.

Maria walked with a limp, but otherwise was prettier than he had expected. As she entered the café, noticed him and gave a shy wave, he allowed himself a shallow moment to appraise a figure that had withstood the test of time with admirable grace, aware that the years of alcohol abuse had kept him sufficiently gaunt that she might think the same. Then he was climbing to his feet, awkwardly introducing himself, and offering her a seat, unsure how much chivalry was required for a woman he had never met.

Maria was a former PE teacher, retired early on disability, an old injury having resurfaced later in life to cut her career short. Slim, currently between cases, felt almost in a position of envy. Although they agreed that black, reheated coffee was better than anything made on that day and ruined by any kind of sugary or creamy pollutant, conversation quickly became troublesome. Slim didn't listen to music. He had no interest in films. The only football team he knew anything about was QPR, and that had nothing to do with the sport. He didn't go to the theatre. He didn't even own a television.

'I used to fish,' he said, remembering a rod he had used perhaps half a dozen times, before managing to lose. 'Do you like fish?' he asked at last, desperate for some last inquiry to fill another uncomfortable silence.

'I have an allergy,' Maria said. 'But I don't mind them in tanks.' She gave a dry chuckle. 'Alive.'

'Like a zoo,' Slim said, for once wishing he was drunk. 'A zoo for … fish?'

'You mean an aquarium,' Maria said, smiling at someone off-camera as though perhaps an imaginary person would be better company. 'I think zoos are cruel.'

Slim was about to point out that since he hadn't been to a zoo since some long-ago school trip then he must by default agree, but it felt like the evening was sliding towards some inevitable anticlimax where they perhaps shared a smile at each other's awkwardness and then silently promised never to meet again. Instead, figuring he might as well ask about the one aspect of Maria that truly interested him, he said, 'How did you get that limp?'

Maria smiled again, more warmly than could have been expected for such a question on a first date.

'Would you believe me if I told you I used to be an acrobat in the Southern Cross Circus?'

Slim smiled in return, perhaps for the first time feeling at ease. 'Since I don't owe you money, and you don't owe me, I have no reason not to. So, you were an acrobat?'

'Specifically the trapeze,' Maria said. 'But the years haven't been kind.'

'Are you talking about for you or for me?'

Maria laughed, and suddenly Slim wondered if a second date wasn't the most impossible of things to consider.

'I fell,' Maria said suddenly, her smile dropping as her eyes led back to some past trauma that still haunted her. 'Someone cut through the rope. It was the night my boyfriend disappeared.'

SLIM'S SCRATCHED and battered Nokia 3310 barely had the capacity to make calls, let alone access the internet, so he went to his local library, borrowed a computer, and looked up Southern Cross Circus.

His initial expectation had been that it might be some Southern Hemisphere version of the Moscow State or Chinese State Circus, both of which he had vague memories of passing through previous areas of residence, even if he hadn't actually attended any shows. He remembered the coupon tickets on the counters of newsagents where he had bought his booze. He was somewhat disappointed therefore to discover that the circus's parent, SCC Ltd had been a minor, and somewhat shady company that had operated in the Midlands for a few short years from the late eighties until its eventual demise in the autumn of 1992, a result of "financial instability", according to the only website he had managed to find where it was mentioned.

What was of more interest, however, was a ten-minute television snippet that had supposedly aired on a local TV channel circa summer 1992, documenting the lives of some of the performers as they prepared to go back on the road. For once the internet failed to turn up the actual clip but merely a mention of its existence. Slim, however, had an old friend who might be able to help.

According to Maria, her accident had befallen her in the autumn of 1992, on the night of the circus's final performance, shortly before it closed for good. By the time of the circus's demise, only a skeleton group of staff and performers had still remained, reflecting the circus's declining popularity, but in the aftermath, many had scattered far and wide. The manager and owner, Lowery Powell, had made a rather clichéd move to the Costa Del Sol, where he had opened a bar in Malaga. A couple of the clowns had moved to the Philippines. One of the acrobats had gone to America and got work as a stunt coordinator in Hollywood. Others had simply transitioned into less lucrative work, and in the thirty years since they had grown old, some even passing away.

It would be a challenge to unearth anyone who knew anything, but first Slim needed to create a picture of what had happened.

'Are we going to go through the motions of pretending this is a second date?' Maria asked as she sat across a table from Slim in a town centre café. 'Or should we just accept this is me ceding to your curiosity?'

'I can buy the coffees,' he said. 'If that makes any difference?'

Maria smiled. 'I'll tell you what I remember. It's long enough ago now that the memories no longer hurt.' She shrugged. 'Not in the way my hip can ache on a rainy winter morning, at any rate.'

'You said your boyfriend disappeared?'

'Yes.' Maria sighed, suggesting the memories of

everything hurt more than she claimed. 'He was there when I went out to perform, and he was gone by the time I fell, because if he ever knew about it, he certainly never came to visit while I was strung up in a hospital bed. And I've not seen nor heard anything from him since.'

'Do you think he's dead?'

'Either very dead or very rich, one of the two. I have to admit, I'd like to know, just for peace of mind if nothing else.'

'Let's start from the beginning. What was his name?'

Maria sighed. She rubbed at a mole beside her left eye as she gazed off into space.

'Jason Felton,' she said. 'He was five years older than me—which, if you really want to know, would make him fifty-three were he still alive.' She chuckled. 'I've got a couple of years before the big five-oh.'

Slim, who had reached that milestone fairly recently himself, just shrugged. 'It's not so bad. I have all the same aches as at forty-nine. So that would have made you eighteen when you were working at the circus?'

Maria gave a shy smile. 'I signed up at sixteen. I had a fake ID I'd bought off a kid at school which I used to get into clubs. Powell just accepted it, but I don't think he cared.'

'There was an age law?'

'For certain acts, I believe. Trapeze was one. Like most things at the circus, it was neither enforced nor regulated. You get some travelling acts where there are families involved, but SSC was a static act which hired its performers on yearly contracts.'

'What do you mean by static act?'

'For most of the year, we had a single location. Customers came to us. It was just outside Birmingham, just to the south of a village called Meadow Cross.' Maria chuckled. 'I think that's why Powell chose the name.'

'I don't know it.'

'It was a pleasant enough place, a few miles southwest of the city, near to a National Trust area called the Cloverdale Hills. We used to walk up there on days off.'

'You said the circus was in a single location. Do you think any part of it is still there?'

Maria shrugged. 'It could be. The big top was on a patch of ground behind a care home called Oak House.' Maria frowned, gave a half smile. 'It was a bone of contention for the locals. There were ... protests.'

'Against the circus?'

Maria shrugged again. 'Look, I was a kid. I was living this kind of rebellious dream, running away to the circus and all that. I was free, and I was in love with this guy I worked with. I didn't really pay attention to what was going on outside the tent. I knew the local people didn't want us there, but it wasn't a big thing for me. It was more of a distraction. A nuisance.' She picked at a corner of the plastic tablecloth that was ripped. 'But I know there were some incidents. Some ... violence.'

3

HIS CURIOSITY WAS like an anchor's windlass, reeling him in. He had a little money to play with after a decent payment for a relatively simple fraud case a few months back, so Slim felt he could afford a couple of days in the Midlands. He liked the peace of the countryside and enjoyed a little solitary walking. He booked a couple of nights in a Bed and Breakfast in the centre of Meadow Cross, within walking distance of the old circus site.

It was a chilly April afternoon when he arrived, parking in a small car park behind the B&B. A kindly old lady whose hair and clothes were so fluffy and white she looked made out of cotton wool fussed him up a staircase to a room on the first floor which had a pleasant view of the rise of the Cloverdale Hills in the distance. After informing him of a few times and rules, she left him to unpack. The bed had creaky springs but looked comfortable, so he took off his boots and lay down for a few minutes while he waited for the provided kettle to boil. Not a fan of B&B coffee, he had brought some of his own, a packet of a dark roasted Mexican blend he had bought fresh from a connoisseur coffee supplier down the road from his current flat. As he stared at where he had left it, in a plastic bag leaning against a stack of cups beside the kettle, he wondered when his life had taken such a turn that he was no longer spooning yesterday's dregs out of a filter.

The date was Wednesday, April 12th. Three days ago he had enjoyed an Easter egg a client had given him, and gone for a stroll in a local park, where he had sat on a bench and watched ducks weaving among reeds in the shallows of a pond. The scar on his side had ached, but not a great deal more than any of the others.

The day had been memorable for one thing, though. He had woken the next day and realised he had gone twenty-four hours without even thinking about a drink.

Although he was yet to take a drink this year—the longest period of sobriety he had managed since serving nine months for manslaughter—the stuff was rarely far from his thoughts. Perhaps he was finally moving on.

The kettle clicked off. Slim got up, made a coffee—thick and black as he liked it best—then stood gazing out of the window at the distant hills.

Unlike many of his previous cases, he had very little opening on this one. Maria's information had been vague, at times seemingly rehearsed, and maybe unreliable. There was the likelihood of sabotage—Maria claimed her trapeze rope had been partially cut through, and a man who had disappeared.

Slim had a reputation for unearthing crimes long lain buried, but he had no idea what he might be able to conjure from this. Maria was convinced Jason had simply run off. It was possible. The circus had closed for good shortly afterwards, while Maria was still in hospital, its doors never to reopen. Lowery Powell had retired with what was left of his fortune and the other performers had dispersed.

Was there a fraud case to be unearthed? Perhaps money laundering, or tax evasion? A case of attempted murder?

As he often did these days when making preliminary investigations, Slim had travelled incognito, booking his room under the name of Mike Lewis. While he felt his fame wholly undeserved, his name was well known among the late-night true crime documentary crowd, and he had found many of them lived in quiet, country villages where otherwise little went on. Slipping a fake ID card into his pocket, he picked up his coat and headed downstairs.

The landlady was chopping carrots in the kitchen. Slim gave a light knock on a door that stood open, and she looked up, put down her knife and picked up her glasses, nestling them into groves on her nose.

'Oh, Mr. Lewis, isn't it? Do you need something?'

Slim gave what he hoped was a disarming chuckle. 'I wanted to ask you for directions,' he said. This might sound like a strange request, but I heard there used to be a circus around here. I work for the BBC's culture department, and I'm looking into the possibility of making a documentary—'

'Oh yes,' she said, squinting into her glasses. 'You're talking about that place that was down behind the care home. I remember taking the boys a couple of times.' She gave a nervous laugh. 'It wasn't my kind of thing, though.'

'Was there something … wrong with it?'

'It was a little seedy for my liking,' she said. 'I can't say I was sad to see it go. I don't think anyone round here was. Not after what happened.'

Slim felt a tickle of something behind his neck. 'What was that?' he asked.

'Well, someone did for those two old ladies, didn't they?' she said in that way a grandmother might when she expected the details were already known.

'I don't follow—'

'Margaret Bellingham and Carrie Thompson. The night of the last performance, someone broke into Oak House and smothered them in their beds.'

4

SUNSET WASN'T until nearly eight o'clock, so Slim set about getting a feel for the village and surrounding area. Meadow Cross was little more than a cluster of houses around a crossroads, although Slim saw no sign of either Robert Johnson or the Devil. He did hear the faint sound of someone practicing blues guitar coming from an open upstairs window, however. Pleasant village streets led away from a central area with a pub on one corner, a Spar on another, with a couple of specialist shops further up the street. From the crossroads, Bromswich Road headed northwards towards Hagley, with Church Avenue and Stowford Road leading away east and west, with Meadow Cross Lane, a narrow road lined with trees, heading south to Belbroughton. A convenient pavement followed the left side of the road which Slim walked along for half a mile or so until he reached the driveway entrance leading to Oak House. Hidden from the road by high hedgerows, Slim paused for just a couple of minutes before heading back to Meadow Cross. Although he was itching to visit the old circus site, he was aware it was on private land and was also a little reluctant to make his presence known so soon. If there were secrets to be uncovered—and he'd found that in these small towns there always were—he needed to dig as deep as he could before the locals started mixing concrete to bury his investigation.

He figured the Spar might be the best place to hunt for local gossip. Behind the counter was a woman of a similar age to Slim, but whose clear skin and grey-free hair suggested she had lived a little better, sitting on a stool while she read a copy of *The Sun*.

'Excuse me,' he said.

She looked up, a little reluctantly, he thought. There was no suspicion in her eyes, just a look of frustration at being disturbed. The newspaper was opened on a double page spread introducing the contestants of some forthcoming beach-based reality TV show.

'Can I help you?'

'Yes, I'm looking for someone who might know a bit about local history. Does Meadow Cross have a village council or something?'

'Let me think … yes, there's the Cloverdale Parish Council, but it's run by an American whose only been here ten years.' She smiled. 'One of those types who just shows up and starts trying to take over everything.'

Someone with a penchant for localism but without an emotional attachment to the village was perfect. Slim tried to look disappointed as he said, 'Well, it would be a start. I don't suppose you have his phone number?'

'Her.'

'What?'

'Her. It's a woman. At least supposedly,' she added with a chuckle. 'Katie Julius. She lives just up Church Avenue. Number 34. I'm sure she wouldn't mind you stopping by. She's always in here, chewing my ear off about dog mess or traffic zones. Who should I say was asking for her in the unlikely event I meet her before you?'

'Sl … ah … Mike Lewis. I'm a researcher. And who should I say sent me?'

'Just tell her Jessica from the shop.' The woman gave Slim a wry smile. 'If she runs me down, be sure to come back and tell me. I'll give you a free tin of beans.'

'Thanks.'

She held her smile as she seemed to warm up a little. 'Always happy to help a stranger.'

'I appreciate it. I'll let you get back to your … ah… business.'

Jessica looked down. 'My money's on Kellie. How about you?'

'Ah … Dave?' Slim said, picking the first name that came into his head.

Jessica chuckled, poking a finger at a bronzed, ab-laden twenty-something, proving Slim had got lucky with his guess.

'Nah, he's got no chance. Can't swim, can he?' Before Slim could answer, she added, 'You have a nice day. See you around.'

'Yes. And thanks again.'

Slim headed out, finding the sun had come out and the day had warmed up almost to the point that he regretted bringing his jacket. He looked around, locating Church Avenue heading off to the east in the direction of the Cloverdale Hills. He passed Cloverdale Parish Hall and found number 34 at the end of a row of nice, upper-class houses.

He felt it necessary to check his appearance in the reflection of a glass bus shelter before opening the gate and walking up a carefully weeded stone path between tidy flowerbeds. The house and its surrounds were almost quintessentially British, right up to the gnome on the front step, the Home Sweet Home doormat and an ornate teapot emblazoned with a Union Jack flag visible behind a frilly lace curtain.

There was a brass knocker which he gave a hard rap, but when a response came it was with a tinny voice through a video intercom beside the door.

'Yes? How can I help?'

'Hello? My name's Mike Lewis. I'm a researcher. I'm doing a piece on rural entertainment and I heard there used to be a circus around here. Jessica in the shop told me you might be able to help?'

'She did, did she?' There was no hint of an American accent, but Slim admitted that through an intercom it would be hard to tell. He was still wondering how to respond when the door swung open with a loud creak. A woman Slim would describe as military stood there, close-cropped greying hair above a hard, taciturn face, a mouth that looked ideal for giving orders. She wore masculine clothes, a button-up shirt under a dark blue sweater, and brown, corduroy trousers. Tinted glasses hid the colour of her eyes. 'Well, you'd better come in, then. I imagine it's local secrets that you're after, isn't it?' She gave a brief laugh that was more of a grunt. 'I'd be happy to tell you what I know.'

5

K<small>ATIE</small> J<small>ULIUS</small> <small>SERVED</small> him thin Darjeeling tea in fragile China cups with images of various royal weddings blended together in a composite. As she set the cups down, she pointed out a set of jubilee crockery in a glass fronted cabinet.

'Limited edition,' she said. 'I got number 14. Would you believe it, that's the date of both my husband's birthday, and his death. I don't think I'd dare serve those even if the Royal Family themselves showed up.' She gave him a brief smile, indicating a joke.

Despite her macho, almost dour demeanour, Slim found Katie Julius instantly likeable. She had a wry sense of humour, like a raincloud which delighted in dousing people. Slim tried to enjoy tea he felt had been made deliberately insipid as she told him tales about her past, and her emigration from the States in search of a less demanding life.

'I got injured in Lebanon in 1982,' she said, confirming Slim's suspicion that she had a military background, and giving him a better estimate of her age as between sixty and sixty-five. She leaned over and pulled up her trouser leg, giving him a momentary view of a wicked scar on her left calf muscle. 'I got a disability discharge, but what was I supposed to do then? Watch TV for the next thirty years?'

'Indeed,' Slim said, making the rare decision to drop a lump of sugar into his tea in the hope of making it taste better.

'I bumbled around for a while doing this and that, then met an Englishman, and over we came.' She spread her arms. 'We were living down south, on the coast. Then Reginald—that was really his name, I mean, you can't get more English than that, can you?—well, he got sick—cancer, the poor soul—and after he passed, well, I couldn't live there anymore. I did think about going home, but only for a minute. We didn't have children, and all my close family have passed on. I looked around for a while, came across this place, and figured it looked all right, you know?'

'And how is it?' Slim forced himself to concentrate while swallowing a gulp of tea, having reminded himself why he never took sugar.

'Oh, it's all right. I keep myself busy. I'm in all the committees, all the clubs. I find people aren't all that friendly, but that's you Brits, isn't it?'

'We have a natural aversion to making friends,' Slim said, eying a pack of decent coffee on a shelf over the kitchen sink.

'Back home you're all buddies within five minutes of moving in,' Katie continued, barely breaking rhythm. 'Over here it can take years to break down all the social walls. Just gotta jump in with both feet, haven't you?'

'Quite,' Slim agreed.

Katie leaned forward. 'Oh, you've finished. Do you want another cup?'

Slim put up a hand. 'Ah … I don't suppose you've got any coffee?'

Katie grinned. 'There's a man after my own heart. This English stuff is weak as anything, isn't it?'

'I usually prefer something a little … ah… stronger,' Slim stuttered.

Katie rolled out the instant rather than the good stuff taunting Slim from the shelf, but it was still an improvement. As Katie sat down, enjoying the company and ready to talk all afternoon, Slim took the brief pause in her monologue to say, 'I was wondering if you knew anything about the old circus that used to operate from the grounds behind the Oak House care home?'

'Before my time,' Katie said, but before Slim felt a measure of disappointment, she added, 'But I've heard some of the stories.' Her smile had gone, and the room felt colder for it. 'It left a bit of a bad taste in the collective mouth, is how I think the locals might put it.'

'I heard a rumour that two residents of Oak House were murdered the night of the final performance,' Slim said. 'One of the performers vanished, and another one was left with severe injuries after a fall that was caused by suspected sabotage.'

Katie leaned forward, fixing him with a drill sergeant stare. 'For a researcher on circus history, you have a keen interest in the more macabre aspects,' she said.

'I … Ah … how did you know I was a researcher?'

'Jessica called me to say you might stop round,' she said. 'We've been friends since I first stumbled into town, even if she is a miserable old mare.' She chuckled, and Slim realised he would have to tread carefully. He had already dropped his guard within a couple of hours of arrival.

'Yes, well, there's a lot of dark stuff associated with the circus, isn't there?'

Katie leaned forward, lowering her voice, although shy of a hidden recording device, there was no way anyone could overhear.

'If I were you, I'd be careful. I didn't have to be here at the time to have felt the lasting effects that place had on this village. Despite all the sun we get, it's like a shadow. People weren't sad to see it gone, for one reason or another. They've moved on with their lives and I think you should leave them be.'

'I understand.'

Katie nodded. 'But you're not going to, are you? I can see it in your eyes.'

Slim had been privy to a number of interrogations during his time in the armed forces, and understood some of the techniques. Now he felt like he was sitting on the other side of a stained metal table in a stone-walled hut in the middle of the Iraqi desert.

'I just have a few more questions,' Slim said.

Katie nodded. 'In that case, from one outsider to another, I'll tell you what I've heard.'

6

THE ST STEVEN'S CHURCH of England was half a mile or so past Katie's place, set on one corner of a crossroads and surrounded by tall trees. Opposite, in a traditional local cottage was a Nepalese restaurant Slim made a mental note to visit for dinner later. The road continued straight past the church toward the Cloverdale Hills, with the righthand junction heading into a jumble of cul-de-sacs, and the left in the direction of a village called Hagley.

Slim entered the churchyard through a covered gate up at the top of a short set of steps, then wandered around for a while, enjoying the peacefulness of the churchyard, before venturing inside for a few minutes. He was getting a feel for the place, soaking up the atmosphere. When he felt ready, he headed around to the rear churchyard, locating the area of the freshest graves.

Of course, there was no guarantee he would find what he was looking for, but the fate gods were smiling and he did, back near the rear churchyard hedge.

He found Margaret Bellingham first, because she had a larger traditional headstone and her grave was well-tended.

Slim made a mental note of the fresh flowers on a grave that was more than thirty years old.

The inscription was simple:

Margaret Mae Bellingham
September 9th, 1921 to September 26th, 1992
Died too soon aged 71
Loving wife, sister, and mother
Forever in our thoughts

He took a digital camera out of his coat pocket and took a photo. There was a lot to unpack already on such a simple headstone. Thirty years on, the possibilities for the flower leaver began at a daughter or granddaughter, but it could just be a kindly former neighbour. He wasn't an expert when it came to plants but from the drooping of the stems he estimated they were three days old, by the look of things some generic dandelions and other wild flowers perhaps picked in the churchyard itself.

Carrie Thompson, on the other hand, was recognised only by a plaque set into the stone wall, a crack running diagonally across its centre, a thumbnail's width circle of stone depressed, almost like the impact of a hammer swung in anger. While there was a metal grill for flowers beside it, it was empty, and crusted with the runner marks of vines that had been cleared away. Simpler, it read only:

Carrie Jane Thompson
Born March 15th 1911
Died September 27th, 1992
Aged 81
Rest In Peace

Carrie had been a decade older, a decade sooner committed to memory, perhaps explaining the lack of flowers, the damage to the inscription plate, and that it was lichen-covered and no longer tended. What Slim immediately noticed, however, was how Margaret's given date of death was a day earlier than Carrie's. Was it simply that their deaths had come either side of midnight, or had Carrie clung on to life after her ordeal?

It was something he would need to find out if his investigation was to proceed further. He left the churchyard and continued up the road, passing a pleasant looking pub at the bottom of the Cloverdale Hills, then carried on until he came to a footpath entrance.

Despite the protestations of his aging and long-abused body, the climb to the top of the central hill was gentle and rewarding, the views over the surrounding countryside spectacular. There was a small stone circle at the top, and he passed dog walkers, mountain bikers, and families with kids wandering along the footpaths. From the top he gazed out at the fields and the villages stretching away into the distance, wondering if there was really enough information for him to begin an investigation.

He had been in this position before, digging for dirt where no one wanted him to, hunting for skeletons better off where they lay. The mystery was gnawing at him though, unwilling to let him go.

After a few minutes of reflection, he pulled out his phone and called Donald Lane, an old friend who now ran an intelligence agency in London.

'Slim, is that you? I'd recognise that heavy breathing anywhere.'

'Hello Don, yeah, it's me.'

'How's the recovery going? Are you back on another case?'

'Getting there,' Slim said. 'And yeah, I might be. Just making a few general enquires.'

'I've heard that one before.'

'Well, we'll see how it goes.'

'What do you need from me?'

'I'm looking for a man named Jason Felton. He disappeared on the night of September 26th, 1992. On the same night, two elderly women, Margaret Mae Bellingham and Carrie Jane Thompson were allegedly murdered in Oak House, a nearby care home. Anything you can find.'

'I'm on it,' Don said. 'Give me a few days.'

7

THE NEXT MORNING Slim drove up to nearby Stourbridge to visit the local public library. He had spent the evening before searching online for any information, but the circus's heyday had ended before the internet age had begun, meaning there was little to be found aside from a couple of passing references. In the library he headed for the microfiche room and began to trawl through old newspapers from the period in question.

His eyes were aching before he found anything at all, and that was simply an advert placed by the circus for a pair of upcoming performances. Dated October 9th, it had been booked before the circus's sudden demise.

Slim, frowning as an idea came to mind, flicked to the front of the newspaper and read down through a list of phone numbers until he found one he was looking for.

Founded in 1985, the Stourbridge News would have been in circulation during the circus's run. Needing coffee, Slim headed to the Clocktower Café outside the library, ordered a coffee and retreated to a corner table. Pulling out his Nokia—which produced looks of

24

amusement from two teens on an adjacent table, he made a call.

'Hello? Yes, my name is John … can I speak to someone in advertising, please?'

'Just a moment, please.'

Slim waited. A moment later, a woman came on the line. 'My name is Janet Cunningham, advertising manager. Do you want to place an ad?'

'I'm sorry to bother you,' Slim said. 'I'm a historical researcher. You weren't working there in 1992, by any chance?'

The woman laughed. 'As though I could escape.'

Slim took that to mean yes. 'This might sound like a strange request, but I'd like to talk to someone who did the advertising for Southern Cross Circus, which used to operate out of Meadow Cross.'

'Well, there's a name I haven't heard in an age. Do you have a number I can call you back on? I can't remember off the top of my head, but I'll have a look and see if I can remember who was in charge of that area at the time.'

'Thanks, I really appreciate it.'

Slim gave Mrs. Cunningham his number and hung up. After finishing his coffee, he went back to the library and continued his search through the microfiche newspapers.

It seemed ridiculous that there would be nothing. After giving up on the news section, he decided to check the announcements pages, and found a brief obituary for Margaret but nothing at all for Carrie. He had begun to feel sorry for the woman; while it seemed that Margaret had been cherished and missed, Carrie had lived and died in anonymity.

He looked up, catching sight of himself in a reflection in a glass sliding door. Fifty, single, no family, no real mark left on the world except for a couple of brief moments of glory that would be remembered longer for what had happened rather than who had been involved … was he heading the same way? Doomed to die in obscurity?

He found himself with an uneasy need to learn more about Carrie Thompson. Nothing at all to do with the case but almost to bring her a little posthumous recognition, to give acknowledgment to a woman who had seemingly passed through life leaving barely a ripple in the water behind her.

He was daydreaming almost, when he looked down, and just to check whether or not he had looked at this page already, he glanced at the page numbers.

And realised something he hadn't noticed before.

Some of the pages were missing.

8

THE LIBRARIAN WAS NEW, and had no idea how long ago the newspapers had been put on microfiche, nor how or who might have removed some of the pages. She suggested Slim contact the newspaper directly to ask about historical copies, while promising to check to see if they had another copy of the missing pages somewhere.

Frustrated, but at the same time aware that he might be uncovering suspicious circumstances that vindicated his decision to come here, he headed back to Meadow Cross. He parked in the B&B's tiny car park then walked across the road to the Spar where he bought a sandwich and a cup of machine coffee. Instead of Jessica, he was served by a teenage boy who resembled her closely enough to suggest they were related.

It was a nice day, cool but with clear skies, so Slim walked up the road, past Katie's place and took his sandwich into the churchyard where he found an old, collapsing bench. He sat down, opened the packet and took a bite of cheddar and pickle, then put the sandwich down beside him and took a sip of coffee. It was weaker than he preferred but better than nothing, and Slim actually found himself smiling. It was rare moments like this that he had once dreamed of, quiet times sat alone without any cares in the world. During his darkest days of alcohol dependance he had often found himself looking at older people sitting alone in the park and feeling an uneasy jealousy. How was life so simple for them when for him it was hard, so complex?

Four and a half months, he reminded himself as he took another bite of the sandwich. When there was so little to be proud of, that was something.

An old man shuffled past, wishing Slim a pleasant day and offering a remark about the weather. Slim smiled and replied that it was a good day for walking. The man laughed and said it was too much for one metal knee and a second arthritic one.

Only after the man had walked on did Slim recall the bunch of wildflowers he had been carrying, their stems wrapped in a damp tea towel as though to keep them from spoiling.

He wanted to let it go, to enjoy the day for a few minutes longer, but the detective in him had too strong a voice. He found himself packing what was left of his lunch away, then following the man around to the back of the church.

Here, the angle of a gentle slope plus a few larger, historical memorial stones gave the graveyard places to hide. Slim made his way towards the back, wondering if the man had reached Margaret Bellingham's grave yet. He was in such haste that he caught his foot on a stray rock and stumbled, recovering himself rather awkwardly and looking up to find the old man kneeling in front of a quite different grave, his previously calm expression now replaced by one of surprise and suspicion.

'Are you all right?'

'I do apologise,' Slim said. 'I caught my foot on something—'

'Well, do be careful. These places can be a minefield. All the uneven turf and everything.'

The man was still staring at him. In an attempt to diffuse the man's growing suspicion, Slim said, 'That's a nice grave. A good send off.'

It wasn't an exaggeration. A polished granite stone with sculpted flowers along the top edge.

'It was the best I could afford,' the man said.

Slim, who hadn't had time to read the inscription, said, 'Your wife?'

The man gave a sad shake of his head. 'My daughter.'

'Oh. I'm sorry.'

The sky was clear, but Slim's clouds had begun to draw in. He wanted to leave the man's presence, to know nothing more. It was coming, though, he knew it.'

'Twenty-seven,' the man said. 'It's too young, isn't it?'

'Yes,' Slim said. 'It is.'

'A drunk driver,' the man said, and Slim closed his eyes. 'She was hit from behind. I like to hope it was quick.'

Slim still had his eyes closed. When he opened them again, the man was gone. For a moment he thought he might have dreamt the whole thing, then he noticed the fresh flowers in the vase, and looked up just in time to see the man's back, as he headed for a path around the side of the church.

Had the man known? Did Slim wear some label that identified him? He had been lucky enough to never hit anyone, but during his worst days, before a two-year ban curtailed him, he had often driven home drunk. He had hated himself every time, but there had always been some excuse. It was raining. It was too far. It wasn't safe to leave the car.

Needing to clear his head again, he turned away from the grave and walked back over to the graves of the two old ladies.

There were fresh flowers in Margaret's vase. Some were wildflowers, but there were a couple of tulips that looked cultivated. Slim frowned, trying to remember where he had seen that type before. There were lots on the flowerbeds along the main road, but he didn't remember seeing any with quite the same color pattern, a streaky yellow and purple.

It was a nice day for a walk. Figuring his tank of bad karma was probably already full, he plucked one of the tulips out of the vase and slipped it into his pocket.

Then, hurrying a little, he headed back around the church to the bench where he had left his sandwich, hoping the birds had left him some.

9

HE TOOK his time walking back to the B&B, taking a stroll along the cul-de-sacs of the little estate, then down a couple of the residential streets around the village's small centre. He failed to spot any flowers similar to the one in his pocket, but his surveillance was limited unless he was in the mood to climb through a few back gardens, and his investigation hadn't quite reached that level of desperation.

However, after stopping back at the B&B to extend his stay by a couple of days, he decided it was time to take a look at the site of the old circus itself.

He walked back down Meadow Cross Lane and turned into the entrance for Oak House, keeping his coat's hood down even though a chilly wind had got up, aware that there might be security cameras somewhere keeping an eye on him, and appearing suspicious would be more likely to make him stand out. The drive was leafy and peaceful, accessing a few private cottages in addition to the care home, meaning his passage might go unnoticed.

Oak House was a pleasant three-storey redbrick building set among landscaped gardens. Slim carried on along the road as it wound around the back of the care home, past a car park, until finally petering out in a stand of brush.

He looked around him. Oak House was behind him, with one of the cottages, a rather unattractive modern garage tacked on to the side, to his right. In front of him was an open area covered with brush which gave the impression of once being clear but having been abandoned. Beyond it was an area of waste ground, a bumpy overgrown area surrounded by tall trees.

Glad he had worn decent boots, Slim started across the open space. In places gnarly trees had grown up, but in others he could tell from how the weeds had failed to take hold that beneath a layer of plant matter was concrete or tarmac. Certain he was crossing the circus's old car park, a few paces further on he stopped at the edge of what must have been the circus's main site.

There was nothing left that he could see now. The land use had changed; in the centre was a pile of cut tree branches, and dried tractor tyre marks were all around, moving back and forth, making turning circles, overlapping each other.

He began to make a circuit of the hedgerow, which bordered a large, flat field beyond. Thick with undergrowth and overhanging trees, he wondered if there might be something lying around, some relic of what had been before buried in brambles and nettles. The best he could find was a rectangle of paper the size of his palm, the one corner not ruined by rain where it had been squeezed beneath a rock showing a faded corner of a big top. Nothing else remained, and the paper had peeled so much that no other details could be resurrected. It was proof that a circus had existed here, but that was all. Slim looked at it one more time, then put it into his pocket.

He was just wondering about climbing further into the hedge when the sound of a snapping branch made him turn. A stern elderly man was striding across the clearing towards him.

'Excuse me. What do you think you're doing?'

Caught off guard, Slim was still weighing up options on a possible response when the man added, 'You do know this is private property?'

Slim tried to untangle himself from a bramble while studying the man. Around sixty, he had an out-of-fashion handlebar mustache that was black striped through with grey, cold grey-blue eyes and overlong hair that had taken a battering from the wind. He wore corduroy trousers beneath a brown jacket that was ill-fitting, suggesting he had grabbed the first one on the rack. On his feet he wore padded slippers, frayed around the edges.

'I apologise,' Slim said, lifting a bramble off his foot. 'I had the impression there was a public footpath through here, but I'm not quite sure of the way.'

The man didn't look in a particularly forgiving mood. 'Well, there isn't,' he said, planting hands on hips. Slim noticed a dark purple bruise on the back of his right hand. 'I would appreciate it if you would kindly leave. I don't want to have to take this further.'

While Slim felt a sense of annoyance at the man's overreaction, at the same time such an adversarial response to his predicament offered a tingling of suspicion.

'It's a nice house,' he said, nodding at Oak House, visible through the trees. 'Are you employed there? If my mother were still alive, I'm sure she'd have been happy there in her final years.'

The man gave a hard shake of his head. 'I live in the cottage over there,' he said, nodding towards the one with the modern garage. 'My brother David runs the house. Not that it's of any business of yours.'

Still attempting to be disarming, Slim said, 'Not for another twenty years at least, all being well.' Then, figuring that this man would probably react badly regardless of what he said, he added, 'Didn't there used to be a circus back here?'

'I suggest you head off back to wherever you came from,' the man said, rubbing the bruise on the back of his hand with the other.

'I'm sorry,' Slim said. 'I'll be going. I do apologise for trespassing. I'll be careful to check for the path in future.'

The man continued to glare at Slim, who stepped past him and made his way back across the clearing to the road. When he reached it, he looked back, expecting to see the man watching him. To his surprise, however, the man was standing with his back to Slim, hands in front of him, regarding the former circus site in a posture that almost suggested longing, as though he were clinging to a lost, nostalgic sense of wonder.

10

Slim headed back to Meadow Cross. It wasn't quite late enough for dinner and the rain that had threatened for the last hour still held off, so he walked back up to the church, taking another scenic route in search of the tulip from Margaret Bellingham's grave.

He was nearly there when his phone rang. He didn't recognise the number, but his phone book only had half a dozen entries anyway, so he took the call, pressing the phone against his ear to hear the voice on the other end over the wind blowing off the Cloverdale Hills.

'Hello?'

'Mr. Lewis?'

'Ah … yes?'

'My name is Cherry Williams. I used to work at the Stourbridge News, in the advertising department. I believe you were asking about the Southern Cross Circus.'

'Yes, I was.'

'I was in charge of their advertising from 1989 to 1992,' she said. 'I heard you work for the radio or something?'

'That's right,' Slim said. 'Thanks for calling me. Would you be willing to answer a few questions?'

'Sure. There's not much I can tell you, but I had to drive over there fairly frequently.'

'That would be great.' Slim checked the clock on his phone's display. 'I'm staying in Meadow Cross,' he said. 'I don't suppose you know anywhere around here that sells decent coffee?'

They met in a cafe in nearby Belbroughton called the Deli. Slim ordered a double espresso—black—while Cherry, a rotund woman in her early seventies, ordered a large latte and a chocolate éclair. Slim picked up the bill, hoping she didn't have too much to say from the way she fawned over the rest of the cakes in the display.

They had to sit outside due to a lack of indoor tables, but a tall privet hedge blocked the wind and most of the noise from the adjacent road.

'It's Mike, isn't it?' Cherry said, eyes flicking between his and the éclair.

'Yes, that's right,' Slim said, preferring to keep his real identity hidden as long as possible. 'I'm just doing some research on the area, and I'd heard there used to be a local circus. And, I mean, that's not really a common thing to have in an area like this, is it? At least not on a permanent basis.'

'Well,' Cherry said, rubbing her hands together and then picking up the éclair in one hand and her coffee in the other as though about to debate which to go with first, 'I think they toured during the school holidays then did regular weekend and evening performances at home the rest of the time. That's what Lowery used to say, at any rate.'

'Lowery Powell?'

Cherry took a bite of the éclair, then said, 'So you know his name?'

Slim shrugged. 'I found it online. What do you remember of him?'

Cherry wiped a piece of chocolate away from the side of her lips. Unable to see herself, she succeeded only in smearing it across her cheek. Slim wondered if he ought to mention it, but just when the dilemma was beginning to make his brain hurt, Cherry reached into her handbag and pulled out a pack of wet wipes.

'He could have been out of a picture book,' she said, not breaking stride as she dabbed at her face. 'He was a total character—what's that word?'

'Caricature?'

'I think that's it. Like, he was loud and jolly and looked silly *without* his top hat, as though he was born for it. I always got the impression it was an act, though.'

'Like he was playing a role?'

Cherry clicked her fingers. Some cocoa powder landed in Slim's cup, but he pretended not to notice.

'That was it. It wasn't all computers like it is these days, you know. At the paper we each had an area and we'd do the ads for that area. Southern Cross was pretty regular but unlike some companies which ran same ad daily or even weekly, Southern Cross changed a lot depending on the season. Sometimes Lowery would send his ads in or stop by, but more often than not he'd call the office and I'd drive down to pick it up. He'd have it ready for me, and I'd bring it back and hand it to the typesetters to put into the next edition.' She chuckled. 'To be honest, I liked getting out of the office. It was constant backstabbing in there. "You're stealing my customers", "that should be on my commission" …' She puffed out her cheeks. 'You've never worked in advertising?'

'Thankfully not.'

'I don't recommend it.'

'So you spent a lot of time down there?'

Cherry nodded. 'I'd say at least once a week during the season, perhaps once a fortnight otherwise. Sometimes he'd offer me a cup of tea, other times he'd simply hand me an envelope with the ad inside.'

'And you always dealt with Lowery?'

'Nine times out of ten. There were other people around but I was never quite sure what they did. You want my honest opinion?'

Slim had thought he was getting it, but it appeared Cherry had a whole other level. For a traditional detective, idle gossip was usually of no use, but Slim always encouraged it. Sometimes a nugget of truth was hidden inside all the exaggerations, half-truths, and casual speculations.

'Tell me anything you like,' Slim said. 'I'm trying to build a picture of the place for my research. I've not had much luck, though. It appears not to have been particularly welcome.'

'You know what?' Cherry said, leaning forward and lowering her voice. 'It was only a rumour, but I heard from a friend on the reporter team that they were warned off covering it. If something major happened, they had no choice or it would look iffy, but the rest of the time it was ignored. And they didn't even run my ads in the Belbroughton and Hagley edition, the one circulated around here. The locals wouldn't buy it.'

Cherry was a potential goldmine. Slim wondered

whether to offer her another éclair now or put it off for another day.

'Can you remember why?' he said.

'People didn't like them,' she said. 'The land, as far as I know, was owned by Oak House. You know, that old people's home nearby?'

'I've seen it,' Slim said.

'But going down there … I mean, it was like out of a film. It felt like a commune. You know, gypsies, or like a cult.'

Her voice had dropped near to a whisper. Even though they were the only customers sitting outside, Slim had to strain to hear over the noise of an occasional passing car and the rustle of the wind through the hedgerow.

'I'd pull up and get out of the car, and there'd be shirtless men just lifting weights in the field, or people in costumes doing practice exercises. I remember there were these two tree stumps and they'd have a wire strung between them, you know, only a foot off the ground, and this one time I was there, this man was walking across, juggling balls or whatever. It was hypnotic. Only just as I found myself entranced, he stepped off, starting swearing and threw the balls on the ground, then pulled out a cigarette or something.' She shook her head and sighed. 'Things like that would happen quite often. I'd be standing outside Lowery's office cabin, just watching them. But if they caught me watching, some of them would glare at me as though I was the strange one, as though I shouldn't be there. And you know what I saw in their eyes?'

Slim just gave a slight shake of his head.

'Total contempt. Like they *hated* me.'

'I imagine it was hard work to keep up your skills in that line of work,' Slim said. 'They were probably just frustrated. Did you notice anything strange about the end, around when the circus shut down?'

'I remember it happened really fast. There was no warning. They were still placing ads for future shows. There was a bit of a kerfuffle that night, the night of the final show—'

'How do you mean?'

'Well, I wasn't there, so take this just as what I heard. A lot of locals didn't like that circus there. On show days it meant traffic jams, noise, and all that. But on other days some of the performers would be out and about in the village. A few of them were troublemakers, and I heard that night a few locals showed up, looking to start something. I don't know what happened, but the next day the circus was closed. Lowery Powell was gone, the performers had packed up and left, and...' She trailed off, gave a shake of her head, then finished what was left of her latte in one long sip.

Slim didn't want to mention the two elderly ladies. He hoped Cherry would, but when she said nothing, he leaned forward and said, 'what happened next?'

Cherry shrugged. 'Oh, it was a long time ago. After the circus closed, I never had a reason to go down there. I heard the big top was pulled down and all the surrounding structures taken away, but I really wouldn't know.'

'Would you like another coffee?'

To Slim's surprise, Cherry shook her head. 'I think I should be getting back. Thanks for the coffee, though, Mike, and good luck with your project. I hope it goes well.'

The bubbly, gossip-hungry demeanour had filtered away, and Slim sensed future calls would go unanswered, voice messages ignored. As she stood up, smiled goodbye and made to leave, he sensed that he had just one last chance to glean any more information.

'These locals who were a little … disgruntled … I don't suppose you have any names? I'd like to get their opinion on what happened?'

She looked back. For a moment Slim didn't think she would answer. Then, with a little sigh, she said, 'I only knew of one. His name was Gavin Thomas. He runs a pub up in Hagley. I'm sorry, I don't remember its name.'

She started to walk away, then paused half turning back. 'If you speak to him … please … don't tell him who told you.'

11

CHERRY'S REACTION made Slim cautious enough to do a little background research on Gavin Thomas before heading off to find him. And the suspicions that had arisen from Cherry's sudden onset of nerves proved justified when a simple internet search brought back multiple newspaper articles and several court filings. It seemed that Gavin Thomas had embarked on quite the life of crime during the nineties, his convictions ranging from car theft to breaking and entering, to possession of narcotics and even GBH. The most recent conviction had been for handling stolen goods in 2001, but after that there was nothing.

Slim called Don.

'I'm still working on it,' Don told him, after Slim had made his latest request and asked for an update on the others. 'I found some information about a Jason Felton from Bath who won a couple of medals in amateur gymnastics. That could be the same guy. I can't confirm it, but I'll drag up what background I can, just in case. Nothing since September 1992, however.'

'And the ladies who died?'

'Not much, I'm afraid. I found some information about a Margaret Bellingham who worked as a teacher in Stourbridge in the sixties, but that's about it so far. I trawled online articles and found a couple of mentions of her name connected with local events. It seems she was well liked, but that's all I have so far. The timeframe involved makes it difficult. I mean, they've already been dead thirty years, and if they died in a care home, it's likely they were out of public view for some time before that. Give me time, though. I'm working my way forwards.'

Slim gave a thoughtful nod. It was possible then that the person leaving the flowers was a former pupil, maybe. 'Did you find Carrie?'

'Nothing yet. I'm still working on it. Give me another couple of days.'

He went back to the B&B, taking a table in the quiet breakfast room downstairs to look over his notes so far. He had been there for half an hour when the landlady appeared and asked if he'd like to order a drink. Remembering what she had told him shortly after his arrival, he called her over.

'If you're hungry, I can rustle something up,' she told him. 'I don't usually cook for guests but you're currently the only one here. Or feel free to order something in.'

'Thanks,' Slim said. 'Actually, I was wondering if you could tell me more about that circus down on Meadow Cross Lane. I've been doing a little research but I'm not getting very far.'

'It was all right if that was your thing,' she said. 'The boys enjoyed it, for what it was.'

She had mentioned them before, but now Slim felt familiar enough with her to ask for more information.

'The boys?'

'Zachary and Simon, my daughter's kids. Sally used to work nights and Mark, well, he went off with some floosy he met at work, so I quite often had them in the evenings.'

Slim sensed a cracking in the lady's floodgates. While he had heard enough family issues to last a lifetime, there might be a clue hidden somewhere. He put down his pen and turned his chair a little.

'I'd love a coffee,' he said. 'And if you're not busy, why don't you join me for a bit? I'd love to know more about it.'

Twenty minutes later, the landlady—whose name Slim quickly learned was Jane Cornick—had got Slim up to speed with her family's history. Much of it was daytime soap opera stuff: Zachary was now a financial analyst working in York, married with two kids, while Simon lived in New Zealand, where he worked as a teacher. Her daughter, Sally, had tragically died of cancer in 2009, and while after Mark walked out she had married a nice man named Brian, he had remarried after widowhood, moving down to London. Jane, whose own husband had died of cancer in 1987—'It ran rampant in his side of the family but I'm hoping the boys have enough of mine in them to avoid it'—still ran the house as a B&B as she had for nearly forty years, while her interaction with what was left of her immediate family had fallen to little more than cards at Christmas and on birthdays, and the occasional phone call.

'That's life, isn't it?' she said, taking a sip from a cup of tea Slim suspected had long ago gone cold. 'We do what we can, but eventually it all just fades away. I'd love to hear more from the boys, but I know they're happy doing what they do, and that makes me happy, you know?'

Slim suspected otherwise, but wasn't about to say.

'You said you heard the two old ladies were smothered,' he said, having been skirting around the question he really wanted to ask for a considerable time, waiting for the right moment.

Jane sighed as she took another sip of her tea. 'I shouldn't have said anything, really. It was always just speculation. There was never an investigation or anything.'

'Who told you?'

'My niece, Vanessa.'

Slim glanced at a clock on a bookcase shelf and realised they'd been talking for nearly an hour, yet this was the first mention of a niece.

'Would it be possible that I could speak to her?'

Jane sighed again. The room seemed to darken, as though someone had left a window open and allowed the evening to come inside.

'Oh, I'm not so sure,' Jane said. 'She's not doing well, is Vanessa. She's not doing so well at all.'

12

'WELL, hello again. I wasn't expecting to hear from you again, Slim.'

'Maria, hi.'

It was never likely to be an easy conversation, when what had initially begun as a potentially romantic introduction had turned into a vehicle for Slim's curiosity, and any chance of romance had left in its wake. All Slim cared about was uncovering the mysteries of Southern Cross Circus and Maria was his main way in.

'Well, I must say, I'm impressed,' she said. 'I didn't expect you to stay the course. When I didn't hear from you, I figured you'd just moved on.'

He shrugged, pressing the phone against his ear. 'I think people would say it's both the source of my power, and my downfall,' he said, feeling a little awkward, as though he was trying to spin her a line. He lowered the phone for a moment, allowing the wind off the Cloverdale Hills to cool the blood reddening his cheeks. When he lifted it again, Maria was back in full flow.

'—leave it up to you, but I don't want to be involved.

I'm not going back to that place, but if you find Jason alive, let me know where he is because I've held a hard slap back for him all these years.'

'To be honest,' Slim said, 'There's nothing left here to see. The circus is long gone. I have questions, though. And any you can answer, might help.'

Maria sighed. 'All right. But if I help you, I want a third date. And I get to pick the place.'

'Sure.'

There was a pause. 'Honestly, I wish you luck, Slim. But I think you're wasting your time.'

'Maybe, but I'm between cases, so there's a little there to waste.'

'Okay, so what do you need?'

'Did you ever encounter a man named Gavin Thomas?'

There was a long pause. Slim began to wonder whether Maria was still there, when a tired chuckle, barely audible, came through the receiver.

'My god, Slim, how deep are you digging?'

According to Maria, Gavin had been a local hard man, infamous around the area for general acts of thuggery and threatening behaviour. Already on the police radar, Lowery Powell had noticed Gavin was a good man to have onside and had hired him to do general door security shortly after the circus had opened. However, a couple of years later, the pair had fallen out over money, and Gavin had been dismissed.

Not one to look away from a fight, Gavin had begun making a nuisance of himself, threatening the staff and performers, and becoming a ringleader of a group determined to see the back of the circus once and for all.

'Was he there the night Jason disappeared?' Slim asked.

'He might have been,' Maria said. 'I don't know, because I was getting ready to perform. I remember hearing that there had been a scuffle in the field out behind the circus. There had been a fight in one of the local pubs the night before, and I suppose they had unfinished business.'

'Between locals and performers?'

'There were a few local hooligans, I suppose you'd say,' Maria said. 'I think they expected the circus staff and performers to be easy pickings, but there were some tough guys around. These were circus people, some who'd worked in the industry their whole lives. There were a few who liked a drink and a scrap on a Saturday night, and we knew there had been trouble with some of the locals in the past. A couple of punch ups, that kind of thing.'

'So Gavin Thomas might have been there looking for trouble?'

'He might have been, but I can't say for sure. I was in my trailer shortly before performing.'

Maria had already given Slim a layout of the circus grounds, and he had drawn a map on a sheet of paper back at the B&B. The big top had taken up the centre of the clearing. Around the back had been a ring of caravans and temporary cabins which homed the staff and performers. Maria had confirmed what Cherry had told him, that while the site was semi-permanent, the circus was designed so that most of it could be packed up and sent on the road a couple of times a year. Around the front, creating a kind of barrier between the car park and the big top, had been a line of stalls and stands: ticket sellers, burgers and hotdogs, a shooting gallery, a fortune teller.

There had even been a play area for children and a small Ferris wheel, enough to entertain people while they waited to enter or took a breather from the main event.

Slim had also made a list of all the grievances locals might have had from such an establishment: congestion, noise, littering, loss of business. He didn't need to look far to find a motive for anything; he could have reached into a magician's hat and pulled out a handful.

At first, the heart of his fledgling investigation had centered around Jason Felton's disappearance and the sabotage of Maria's trapeze act. As it picked up pace, it had collected the suspicious deaths of two old ladies along the way, and now Slim found himself wondering what had been the root cause of the circus's downfall.

'Was it busy, that last night?' Slim asked.

'Three quarters full,' Maria said. 'That was about normal.'

'Was the business doing well?'

'I don't know,' Maria said. 'I got paid what Lowery said I'd be paid, and the work was no harder than I expected. Me and Jason were an item, and everything was grand.'

'Did Jason ever give any indication that anything was wrong?'

'No, never. I mean, we never had that kind of conversation. We were both young. I thought we were in love. Despite what happened, I'm still not convinced that we weren't.'

13

WHILE NOT FEELING QUITE the enthusiasm for an early morning hike up the Cloverdale Hills, a morning stroll was in order, so Slim found himself wandering around Meadow Cross's residential streets with the sun just rising above the roofs of the houses to the east.

He had found it difficult to sleep. In his hands wasn't so much as a knot but a jumble of loose pieces of string, somehow needing to be tied together.

He had called Don again, but his usually affable former comrade in the Armed Forces had politely asked for a little more time.

He had a defunct circus, its owner now living overseas. A missing person, an act of sabotage. Two dead elderly women and a disgruntled local thug.

It could all be connected, or it could not. And Slim could be running on the wrong tracks entirely. Jason might have just run off. Maria's trapeze line might have just broken, an act of negligence for sure, but nothing suspicious. And the two old women, in a care home as they had been, might have just died.

It occurred to Slim that the one lead he hadn't pursued so far was to try to contact the circus's former owner himself. Lowery Powell had taken his money and flown out to start a new life on the Costa Del Sol, so Maria had said.

But what if Maria was wrong?

During the night's sleepless middle hours Slim had done a search online for Lowery Powell, but aside from a few old circus articles, there was nothing. Like Jason Felton, it seemed he had disappeared too. From what Maria, Cherry, and others had said, running a quiet bar in Spain didn't fit a man of such a boisterous, overbearing personality. In Slim's experience, people could bend and shape, but they couldn't intrinsically change. Quiet people stayed quiet and loud people stayed loud. Even if Lowery Powell had turned his garrulous nature to bar ownership, the showman would have stood out, and in the modern world, that would have been through social media. Yet, Slim had found nothing. He would need Don's expertise to make sure, but it appeared Lowery Powell had headed over to Spain and then disappeared.

Of course, it was possible he could have changed his name, but again that would have gone against his natural showman's instinct. He would have wanted to return his name to past glories, not start anew.

Slim was nearly back at the B&B when he saw Katie Julius walking along the other side of the road. Wearing a headband and with a flashing GPS watch on her wrist, she seemed happy enough to take a break from her power-walking when he hailed her.

'Still here, then?' she called in an unnecessarily loud voice, when she was still halfway across the street. I thought you would have gone by now. There can't be that much to keep you interested around here.'

'I like the peace and quiet,' Slim said. 'I've found it to be rare.'

'I wouldn't give it up for the smoke,' she said. 'There are a few properties around if you're interested.'

'Out of my price range, unfortunately.'

'And I imagine your work keeps you on the road,' Katie said. 'What is it you do again?'

'Research,' Slim said, remembering that she knew him as Mike Lewis.

'And how is that going? Anything I can help you with?'

Slim paused, wondering how much he could trust her, how quickly rumours of his questions might spread.

'I'm still researching that old circus,' he said at last. You wouldn't by any chance know a local man by the name of Gavin Thomas? I'm looking for people who were involved with Southern Cross Circus and I heard he used to work there.'

It was a risky link but a better one than revealing what he'd heard about Gavin's criminal past.

To his surprise, Katie lifted an eyebrow and said, 'Oh, really? Yes, of course I know him. He owns the Pig and Pen up in Hagley.' She chuckled. 'Despite its name, it's the nicest pub in the area. He's rarely there, though. If you want to speak to him, you'd be better off going up to St Steven's on a Sunday morning. He's the current part time vicar. Round here we know him as Reverend Thomas.'

14

'SLIM?'

'Hi Don. Any updates?'

'Some. I've got you some images of Jason Felton. They're not the best, but it's a start. They're from a gymnastics magazine circa 1990.'

'Great. Can you email them?'

Don chuckled. 'You have email now? What kind of a seismic shift is this?'

Slim shrugged. 'I'm trying to modernise. It's not my first, of course, I'm not that bad. It's just the first for which I could remember the password for longer than a week.'

'That'll save some time. Let me know your address and I'll send them over. That's not all, though.'

'What do you have?'

You know what facial recognition software is, don't you?'

'You'll have to be more specific, I'm afraid.'

'Well, times are changing, I imagine for everyone but you. I've run those pictures through software that trawls publicly available content on the web. These days there's a lot, what with social media such a mainstay in people's lives. It picks up similar images and assigns them with a percentile value based on how closely they match.'

'You're losing me, but go on.'

'Anyway, I think I've found him.'

'Jason? Are you serious?'

Slim felt a prickle run down his arms. What would Maria say when he found out her former boyfriend was still alive?

'I found some pictures posted online in 2018,' Don continued. 'Helpfully, there were a series of pictures covering various stages of his life. While the percentage likelihood of a match drops the more recent the photos are, the early ones are in the high eighties and early nineties. Considering the poor quality of the source photos, that's an excellent match. Something well worth investigating, at any rate.'

'That's fantastic, thanks, Don. Does he live near here?'

'That's the problem. The pictures were from a memorial page posted online. The man in question died in February 2018 of a heart attack, according to the page. He was only forty-seven, but again, the age adds up, doesn't it?'

'Can you send me the link?'

'I'll put it in with the pictures. One more thing, Slim.'

'Yes?'

'Jason's family lived overseas, in New Jersey, according to a couple of location tags on the later pictures. They were posted by his son. However, he's quite active online and leaves an easy trail to follow. He came back to the UK in 2020 for work and now lives in Shrewsbury. That's not so far from you, is it?'

15

THE LEADS WERE BEGINNING to build up. Slim, sitting at the desk in his room at the B&B, drew lines across a sheet of paper, connecting names and events.

Jason had changed his name to Charlie Blondin. A brief internet search had revealed Jason's lack of inventiveness: a man named Charles Blondin was a former circus performer from the 19th Century who became famous in 1859 for the first of many tightrope walks across Niagara Falls. So audacious was his feat that he even stopped to drink from a bottle of wine halfway across, and later repeat performances included pushing a wheelbarrow, carrying his manager, and taking a small stove with him to cook an omelette.

Unlike his new namesake, it appeared the man formerly known as Jason had lived a quiet life after his circus days were over. The memorial page mentioned a family accounting firm, and a side business in landscape gardening.

His son, Steve Blondin, who Slim had seen in some of the pictures, lived in a shared house in a quiet Shrewsbury suburb, and worked in a local bank. Slim was itching to talk to him, but was well aware he could be opening doors Steve didn't even know existed.

No one moved overseas and changed their name without reason. Without evidence that Jason had been involved in a crime, however, Slim was just digging holes that didn't need to be dug. He needed more evidence before he began to confront people. He needed to speak to people who had been at Southern Cross Circus the night Maria's act had been sabotaged, and two old ladies in the building next door had died.

He didn't want to press Jane Cornick for more information, but luckily her niece was easy to find. Jane had a rarely used Facebook page open to public view, and there was only one Vanessa listed in her friends. Vanessa's page, also public, hadn't been updated in a couple of years, but had a workplace listed, a Birmingham city centre bar called Tony's. Slim drove into Birmingham, then, after a few stumbling requests for directions, which made him briefly question his decision to neither upgrade his trusted Nokia to a smartphone nor buy a local map, he arrived at the door to a shabby street corner establishment.

It was easy to make assumptions from the downtrodden, litter-strewn locale as to what might go on inside, but Slim preferred to reserve judgment until he'd managed to speak to a member of staff. He was unable to locate a back entrance and no one answered his knock, but luckily there was a greasy spoon café across the street from where he could observe. He took a window seat, ordered a coffee and a plate of bacon and eggs as a late breakfast, then settled down to wait.

He was on his third coffee when a brewery truck pulled up outside. The driver got out, made a phone call, then shortly afterwards the door opened and a heavyset man wearing only a vest and jeans stepped out onto the street, a cigarette dangling from his mouth. He waved at the driver to back the truck up, then together they began to unload barrels of beer onto a trolley and wheel them inside.

Slim took his chance. He paid up then wandered across the street. Pulling out his phone, he held it to his ear and pretended to be finishing a call just as the man in the vest came back outside, followed by the truck driver with the trolley.

'Excuse me?'

'Yes, mate?' The man sounded friendlier than he looked, with forearms powerful enough to crush chests.

'This is Tony's, isn't it? I'm looking for someone called Vanessa Richards. She works here, doesn't she?'

It was a simple interrogation trick, looking for an automatic confirming response rather than giving the man a chance to deny knowledge of her.

To Slim's surprise, the man lifted his arm and looked at a battered watch.

'She's not here now but she should show up in about twenty minutes. Don't keep her too long, though. Big party last night and the place got wrecked.'

Slim's head had been filled with images of drunken punters, pole dancers and sordid after-hours trysts. As it dawned on him what the role of Vanessa's employment was, he must have looked surprised, because the man in the vest chuckled.

'In fact, if you've got half an hour, grab a mop and bucket and help out. I'll give you twenty quid.'

∿

Vanessa showed up a short while later. The smell of stale alcohol both enchanted and horrified Slim to a point that he couldn't bring himself to go inside, so waited out on the street for her to arrive, even though the man in the vest offered him a sneaky half a lager for courage, 'If you're planning to ask her out or something.'

Slim didn't understand the man's apparent mirth until he saw Vanessa walking up the street a few minutes later. It was unkind to say she was unattractive, but the years had been hard. There had been no pictures on her Facebook page and Slim understood why.

She was of average build, thin but in a scrawny way, her hair prematurely grey, her face lined, her skin mottled and uneven. Her nose was slightly flattened, a sign of having been broken and one eye socket was slightly misshapen, indicating a past trauma injury. Slim immediately felt a pang of guilt, and as she passed by without even looking up, heading into the club, he considered walking away. Then, a voice shouted, 'You see that guy out there waiting for you?', and he knew it was too late.

He was standing on the pavement, feeling absurd, when Vanessa leaned out of the door, looked him up and down, and said, 'What?'

There was no point trying to soften things, and it was time he came clean. He gave her what probably looked like a tired smile and said, 'Vanessa Richards? My name is John Hardy, but most people call me Slim. I'm a private detective. I'd like to talk to you about what happened at Oak House on the night of September 26th, 1992.'

She stared at him. Then, her downcast mouth began to widen. For a moment Slim thought she might smile, then she lifted a hand, rubbed her bad eye, and started to cry.

16

Vanessa had little time to talk but they exchanged mobile numbers. While he waited for her to call, he wandered across town, finding a library where he asked about microfiche copies of the *Stourbridge News*. To his disappointment he was told to visit the Stourbridge Public Library, or appeal directly to the newspaper. He went outside and called the newspaper, only to again be told that he should visit the Stourbridge Public Library, where microfiche records were held.

With a wry smile, he headed up the street to a chain store café, where he sipped a bland straight coffee while planning his next move.

When his phone rang, to his surprise it was Don instead of Vanessa, whom he had expected.

'Not much, Slim, but I've got something,' Don said. 'You'd be amazed what records get saved. In search of this Lowery Powell, I searched flights to the Costa Del Sol from September and October 1992. I managed to get a copy of a boarding pass in the name of a Powell, Lowery, on September 29th, flying from London Luton at 19:45, landing in Malaga at 21:35. The flight departed on time, and the boarding pass was activated, meaning our man at least got onto the flight. I discovered that landing cards are also saved, so I've requested a copy of that from the relevant authority. It'll take a few days, though.'

'Thanks, Don, that's great.'

'I'm still investigating Carrie Thompson. Not finding anything yet, but I haven't given up.'

'I appreciate it.'

Don hung up. Slim took a deep breath. So, he could at least now prove that Lowery Powell had fled the country. Where he had gone from there was anyone's guess, but short of flying to the Costa Del Sol and trawling the myriad bars himself, Slim had no other way to hunt for an onward trail. Still waiting on Vanessa, he decided to head back to Meadow Cross.

It was too early to go back to the B&B, so he wandered around the village, finding a footpath that led through the fields behind Oak House. It bordered the wrong hedge of the field directly behind, but there was enough of a muddy animal track that he could use misdirection as an excuse should the need arise.

At the back of the waste ground behind Oak House, however, the hedge was too thick and the trees too tall for him to even see over. Quite what he was hoping to find, he wasn't sure, but nevertheless felt a sense of disappointment. Instead of turning back, he decided to do a loop and continued onwards. As he rounded the corner of the field and found himself on a farm track that joined the entrance road to Oak House, the hedgerow dropped low enough that he could see into the nursing home's gardens.

And there, to his surprise, was a flowerbed teeming with the same type of tulip that was now shrivelling and drying in his coat pocket.

17

IF IT WAS a member of staff laying flowers at the grave of Margaret Bellingham thirty years after her death, why Margaret and not Carrie?

It was time for Slim to step his investigation up another level. He headed back up Meadow Cross Lane and down Church Avenue to St Steven's. By the time he arrived it was past six o'clock. The church was locked but a notice in a bulletin board cabinet by the main entrance mentioned an evening service labeled only as "Monthly Sanctuary Meeting", starting at seven o'clock. Slim went across the road and had an early dinner in the Nepalese restaurant on the corner, taking an upstairs window seat from where he could observe the church entrance. Just after half past six a car drove past, pulling in to a small car park to the church's side. A man got out, walked down the road, opened the bulletin board cabinet with a key, then adjusted a couple of the notices inside, taking some expired ones down and adding a couple more. Slim watched, trying to get an impression of the man, who was tall with wide, powerful shoulders but who walked slightly stooped as though embarrassed by his size. When the man finally turned around, pausing to observe the road junction as though waiting for a crowd to arrive, he revealed a thick, greying beard, leaving most of his face a mystery.

Aware the service was about to start, Slim reluctantly finished up a meal far better than what he was used to, paid and headed across the street, just as a scattering of regular parishioners began to appear.

He entered the church and sat near the back, but close enough to the other attendees so as not to attract unwanted attention. The congregation showed a familiar decline in church attendance that was commonplace across the country, with barely a dozen people in attendance. Aside from Jessica in the shop and her son, who sat together on a front pew, there were no other familiar faces. Slim kept his head down as Gavin Thomas walked up to the pulpit, hoping neither would turn and see him.

The service turned out to be a support group for those who were undergoing trauma or had overcome it in some way. After a brief sermon, a couple of readings by parishioners, and a couple of hymns, people were invited to share stories of overcoming personal struggle. After one woman stood up and recounted a victory over cancer, another how she had overcome the tragic loss of a child, to Slim's surprise, Gavin Thomas himself returned to the pulpit, took off a pair of glasses, cleared his throat and began to speak.

'You all know me as Reverend Thomas,' he said, 'And you treat me with the respect my title commands. Once upon a time, however, recently enough that I can remember it clearly, I was known by a number. A prisoner number.'

He went on, detailing how finding religion in prison had steered him away from life as a petty criminal, and that since last leaving prison in 2002 his life had remained on track. He thanked the Lord for his deliverance from sin, then looked around, inviting new attendees to share their stories.

His eyes fell on Slim, who had been trying to stay inconspicuous.

'Friend, I've not seen you here before. Would you like to share?'

Slim would have liked to have run away, but all eyes were turning towards him, their expectant stares locking doors, closing escape routes.

He stood up, cheeks burning. What could he say, bar the truth?

'I … I like a drink,' he said slowly, glancing around the assembled faces, wondering how he could water it down enough to wash their eyes away. 'I like too many drinks.' He remembered how he had felt at the smell inside Tony's this morning, how it had threatened to first consume him, and then tear him apart. 'Recently … I've been able to control it, but I'm only ever one drink away from oblivion. I think … I'll always only be one drink away.'

Reverend Thomas gave a sage nod. 'Thank you for sharing. What's your name, friend?'

'John. John Hardy.'

As the words left his mouth, he heard Jessica whisper something to her son, loud enough for other parishioners to hear. As the boy frowned, Slim realised his mistake, how he had been disarmed by allowing his greatest weakness to regain a brief hold of him. While he might currently be controlling the drink itself, he had failed to keep the doors it opened closed, and now his secret was revealed.

Mike Lewis, trying to remain unnoticed, was a lie.

Rumour mills would already be cranking up, fingers would start making internet searches, and within hours the whole village would know there was a private detective—one renowned enough, even if it pained him to admit it, to have been featured in television documentaries—walking among them.

How many people would be willing to speak to him now?

18

HE NEEDED to get away from Meadow Cross for a while, so he checked out of the B&B the next morning and headed north to Shrewsbury, where he took a room in a cheap, out-of-town chain hotel.

There, in the confines of a bland but functional room with a view of a traffic roundabout, he wondered whether he should let the investigation die. If there were secrets to be uncovered in Meadow Cross he had just pushed them further into the dark by mistakenly revealing his. Or had he? Might there be people who would talk to him now that they knew his true purpose?

He went outside, across the busy main road to where a cycle path led along the River Severn. For a couple of hours he let his mind drift, trying to decide what to do, but his thoughts kept coming back to the investigation, and by the time he returned to the hotel a little after lunchtime, he knew there was no way he could let it go. He might have barely stirred the waters, but he had stirred them enough to create a pattern. And he wanted to see more.

Back at the hotel, he found the address Don had given

him for Jason Felton's son, then drove across town. After all, he could lie to himself and claim Shrewsbury had been a conveniently located bolt hole, but it was more than that.

It was the next stage.

Steve Blondin, son of Charlie Blondin, formerly known as Jason Felton, lived in a shared house in Shrewsbury's town centre, next door to a bakery where Slim bought a sausage roll for lunch. When he knocked on Charlie's door, the half-eaten sausage roll held in his other hand in a bid to make himself less threatening, it was answered by a disheveled student-type who appeared to have roused themselves from bed for the purpose. When Slim asked if Charlie was home, the girl first shrugged, then called his name over her shoulder, then shrugged again and said he must be at work. When Slim asked where that might be, he was told the name of a bank in the town centre. Slim thanked the girl, then located the bank, where he made a show of checking his accounts at an inside ATM while looking for Steve among the visible workers. Although not working on the counter, he did catch a glance of the man walking around in the back, working in some non-customer contact role. Unable to speak to him without creating a scene, Slim retreated outside, found a café, and took a corner seat.

He had some time to kill before closing time, so took out the papers of information he had arranged so far and read through them, looking for anything he might have missed.

So far, he had little to work with. If he could prove Jason Felton's identity, that was one thing, but nothing much went beyond there. Was he connected to the deaths of the old women or the sabotage of Maria's trapeze? What motive might he have had, and how could Slim ever prove it?

Then there was Vanessa, from what Slim could gather, the original source of the rumour that Margaret Bellingham and Carrie Thompson were murdered. He picked up his phone and called her number, but again no one answered.

Perhaps it was just a fantasy, made up by someone surely too young to have ever worked at Oak House, a fantasy that had rolled on and become heavier until it had consumed its originator with its weight. But how did that explain the missing microfiche pages?

With nothing to do except wait, Slim killed some time with a little of his own research. He had brought his laptop, so he took it out of his bag, opened it on the tabletop and connected to a store Wi-Fi signal. He looked up Oak House, finding a website advertising its services. Under the ABOUT section, it listed the owner as a David Bellingham. Slim gave a surprised chuckle at his own incompetence when it came to checking basic information. It was highly likely David and Margaret were related. If the David who owned Oak House was of a similar age to the brother Slim had met, it made sense that Margaret was their mother, or grandmother at a stretch.

It also explained the flowers; most likely David or perhaps his brother still held the woman's memory in high regard. And it also explained the lack of flowers for Carrie, nothing more than a long departed resident.

Slim dug deeper, searching for online profiles and social media. While Oak House had a couple of social pages, they were nothing more than advertising spaces containing photos of gardens and empty bedrooms. He did manage to find a business page profile for David, but it listed nothing more than a very brief bio and an address and web link to Oak House.

Frustrated, Slim closed down his laptop, and was about to call Don for an update when he realised it was nearly five o'clock. Slim packed up and paid, then walked up the street to observe the bank. Shortly after a local church bell began to chime, a side door opened and bank staff began to file out. They moved away in pairs or small groups, wearing jackets and hats to ward off the evening cold. Slim looked for Steve and spotted him near the back, one of the last to leave. As the others moved off, Steve set out on his own, walking briskly up the street, a sense of purpose in his stride.

Across the street, Slim followed.

He had the fallback plan of knowing where Steve lived, but it would be better to catch him alone. Slim hoped Steve might stop off in one of the shops yet to close, but to his surprise, as he came to a corner, Steve jogged across the road and through the door of a glitzy wine bar where optimistic staff were defying the cold by setting up tables outside.

Slim's hopes deflated. Perhaps Steve was meeting someone, going on a date. If so, Slim would have to put off his attempt at contact for another day. As he reached the outside of the bar, however, he looked in through windows strung with fairy lights at a gaudy interior where fake candles flickered on wicker tables surrounded by cane chairs, and saw Steve sitting alone at a room-length bar backed with enough spirit optics to make Slim weep. A young barman handsome enough to draw a crowd on his own set a bottle of red and a single glass down in front of Steve, who hunched over the bar like a man clinging to the side of a capsizing ship. As the barman walked away, Steve lifted the bottle by the neck and sloshed wine into the glass.

Slim gave a slow, knowing nod. He knew the motion all too well. Only drinkers poured with the neck. It was a disrespectful but resigned gesture, one borne from inevitability. Slim didn't know why Steve had chosen this particular bar, but he could tell without needing to know that the bottle was the cheapest on the menu. Perhaps Steve preferred a warm bar to a park bench or his own living room. Location was a choice; the means was not.

Slim took a deep breath and went inside. No one smiled at him as they might have at Steve; at his age and with his beard and thick, tatty coat he was deeply out of place. Hours before dress codes might have been required however, Slim took a seat at the nearly empty bar. He ordered a bottle of beer, keeping his hands on his knees as the barman set it down. He had thought to carry it over, to look casual, but as he stared at it, he knew the motion would have set off the old chain. Carrying would have led to the inevitable sip, which would have led to finishing everything within a few seconds, a hand raised to order more, oblivion, maybe violence, certain regret. Instead, he left it where it stood, got up from his stool and walked down the bar to where Steve sat, staring into space, one hand gripping the neck of the bottle, the other the stem of a half full wine glass.

'Excuse me,' Slim said, sitting down on a bar stool. 'Are you Steve Blondin?'

At first Steve didn't react. Slim studied him in profile, a thin, wiry man, his jaw a little receding, giving him a jowly look despite being obviously underweight. His eyes were downcast, his hair prematurely thin.

'Who are you?' he said, not looking up.

'My name is John Hardy. I'm a private detective. I'm looking into the disappearance of a man named Jason

Felton. I believe he might have been your father, having changed his name.'

There were many ways Steve might have reacted. But the one in which he did took Slim so completely by surprise that he had no time to react. He was still studying the man's face when something hard struck him in the side of the head, and his vision became red-washed in the moments before he went crashing to the floor.

19

WHEN HE OPENED HIS EYES, he found a female police officer sitting beside his bed. She initially looked surprised to see him, rearranging and closing a copy of the *Daily Telegraph* open across her knees.

'Oh, you're awake. Hang on, I'll call a nurse.'

She was gone before Slim could even get a name, but a few seconds later she reappeared with a nurse in tow, and for the next few minutes there was a flurry of activity around his bed as nurses and doctors came and went, checking charts and adjusting machines. The WPC was reluctantly shooed out into the corridor and a young doctor took her place by Slim's bed.

'Welcome back,' he said. 'My name is Doctor Bates.'

'What happened to me?'

'You were hit over the head with a wine bottle. You were unconscious when you arrived at hospital, so you were kept sedated overnight while we checked you for any brain injury.'

'And the results?'

'You'll be fine. You were lucky, and there's no long-term damage. We'll need to run some more tests but you should be able to walk out of here in a couple more days. I think the police need to speak to you, though.'

'Okay, send them in. Let's get it over with.'

The doctor smiled and left, and shortly after, the WPC reappeared.

'My name's WPC Jenna Cale,' she said. 'We need to talk to you about what happened. We have identified the suspect in your assault and taken him into custody pending an investigation and charge. Everything was recorded on CCTV inside the bar, plus there were a couple of eyewitnesses. The man in question claims you were harassing him, but it would be hard to prove that in court, based on the evidence available.'

'I don't wish to press charges,' Slim said.

'You don't? You suffered a serious injury, Mr. Hardy.'

'It was a misunderstanding.'

WPC Cale tried to argue her point, but Slim understood the law and pressed his case. In the end, she shook his hand, wished him a full recovery and told him to get in touch with the police if he changed his mind.

A couple of days later, Slim was discharged. He had a bruised crown, a pulled muscle in his neck from an awkward twist during the fall, and was told to see a GP if he experienced any blurred vision or recurring headaches. Otherwise, he had recovered well enough that the doctors expected no further issues.

The hospital had checked his wallet for identification and found a hotel door card. Upon receipt of the information, the police had informed the hotel of his situation. When he arrived back at the hotel, Slim found his room had been kept, the room charge waived. Slim thanked the manager and booked a couple more nights.

He had unfinished business in the area.

It had worked in the past, so rather than attempt a direct confrontation, he wrote Steve Blondin a letter, dropping it through the letterbox the morning after his discharge. Then, with his neck and head still aching from the assault, he found a public library and whiled away the day with some online research.

He didn't expect to receive a response so quickly, but as he was walking back to his hotel just after six p.m., his phone buzzed.

I'm sorry. You caught me by surprise. I reacted badly.

The message had to be from Steve. Slim messaged back: *I didn't mean to startle you. You're not in any trouble. I was looking for your father. Can we talk?*

No reply came for some minutes. Slim was beginning to think Steve had bailed on him when his phone buzzed again.

Ok. Where?

Is there a café near your place?

There's a greasy spoon. Al's Bites.

I'll meet you there at 7. Ok?

Sure.

20

AL'S BITES was a downstairs corner place which felt a lot bigger on the inside than it looked from the outside. An American style counter bar was surrounded by Formica tables and metal framed chairs. Shrewsbury Town Football Club memorabilia hung from the walls.

Steve was already lurking at a table in the far back corner, facing the door, head lowered like a cornered animal. Slim walked over, pulled out a seat, then nodded at the menu.

'Do you mind if I eat?'

Steve shook his head.

'Do you want anything?'

Steve looked about to shake his head again, then gave half a shrug. 'A bacon bap, if you're buying.'

'And a coffee? I think coffee.'

For the first time Steve gave a nervous smile. 'Sure.'

Slim went over to the counter and ordered, then came back and sat down.

'Thank you for not pressing charges,' Steve said. For the first time Slim noticed an American accent, although it was slight, as though he'd grown up in near silence. 'The police said—'

'You swing like a girl,' Slim said with a smile. 'Wouldn't have made much of a baseball player.'

He had attempted to make a joke, but Steve suddenly burst into a confusing mixture of sobbing and laughter, rubbing his forehead with one hand while clawing at the tabletop with the other. Slim glanced over his shoulder, wary of attracting attention from other customers. Thankfully the café was empty aside from a couple of men almost out of sight around the counter corner, neither of whom paid Slim or Steve any attention.

'I'm sorry, I didn't mean to react like that, I just … his name triggered me.'

Slim, who had experienced things during his one combat tour of Iraq aged eighteen which still gave him nightmares, recognised in Steve what people these days called PTSD.

'I didn't mean to alarm you,' he said. 'I was just looking for some information.'

'What did you say your name was?'

'John Hardy. But people call me Slim.'

'Huh. Why's that?'

A little personal insight might help to disarm Steve, make him more inclined to talk.

'It involved a situation during my Armed Forces days. There was this section of metal pipe we were unloading from a truck outside Baghdad. We—'

'You were in Iraq?'

'First Gulf War.'

Steve gave a respectful nod. 'Huh. You don't look old enough.'

'I wasn't. I'd just turned eighteen. I'm fifty now.'

'That must have messed you up a bit.'

Slim shrugged. 'It was what it was. I only did one active tour. I did a bit of base work after that, back in the UK, then got myself a dishonourable discharge.'

'Why?'

'I tried to kill a man I thought was sleeping with my wife. I went after him with a razor blade.'

'What happened?'

'It was the wrong man. Luckily, I was too drunk to cause any damage. I got off lightly. My wife went off with the man she was really sleeping with. A butcher called Mr. Stiles. I never learned his first name.'

'Did you have any kids?'

Slim closed his eyes, rubbing his temple, trying to erase a memory that haunted him more than any other.

'No,' he said quietly, a lump in his throat.

If Steve had more questions, they were cut off by a man Slim guessed was Al arriving with their food. He set it down with a smile, pointed out a tray of condiments on a corner table, and went back behind the counter.

'You came back to England to get away from his memory, didn't you?'

Steve looked surprised. 'What are you, psychic?'

Again, disarming himself might help Steve to open up.

'I was involved in interrogations,' he said. 'I was too young and inexperienced to lead, but I watched others. In most cases, the prisoners were happy to talk. It felt like all we had to do was give them permission.'

'Sounds more interesting than working in a bank.'

Slim shrugged. 'I don't know. I imagine both have their ups and downs.' He took a sip of coffee, nodding with approval. Al made the best coffee since yesterday's filter. 'Can you tell me about your father?'

Steve stared off into space, brow furrowed. 'He ... he was strict,' he said after a long pause. 'Nothing I could do was right. But it was always behind closed doors. To everyone else he was a total god in the community. Everyone loved him.'

'Is that why you wrote such a glowing memorial piece? That's how I managed to find you.'

'I had to. No point in trashing him after his death, was there? No one would believe me, anyway. Might as well send him off the way everyone looked at him.'

'Then draw a line under it by moving overseas?'

'I couldn't stay in that town. Getting back slaps every damn day from people who thought they knew my father. The truth was, none of them knew him. I didn't really know him either. One day he'd be a great guy, taking me fishing or out to ball games, the next he was ripping into me, tearing up my school work, taking off his damn belt—'

He thumped the tabletop hard enough that Slim looked around, but the two other customers had left and Al was busy in the kitchen.

'What about your mother?' Slim said.

'I don't think she was sad to see him go,' Steve said, not looking up. 'She remarried within a year and moved to the next town. She offered me the house if I paid a fair rent, but I refused. I couldn't stay there. I couldn't even sleep after he died because it was as though he'd moved upstairs into my head. I drifted for a bit then moved over here. He still had an English passport. It was easy to get a visa.'

Slim gave a thoughtful nod. 'Do you know why I'm looking for him?'

'Did he kill someone? It wouldn't surprise me. I never felt that he was a psycho, but he had a ruthless streak, that's for sure.'

Slim reached into a bag set at his feet and pulled out the photos Don had sent him of Jason as a young gymnast.

'Is this your father?'

Steve leaned over them and frowned. 'Yeah, looks like him. I've never seen these before. Everything before I was born was basically a mystery. He never spoke about being a kid, except in abstract terms. No grandparents on his side, nothing like that. Mum said he told her he was an orphan, brought up in a foster home in England, something like that. That was it. I could hardly ask.'

'His name—the one I've learned, at any rate—was Jason Felton. He grew up in southern England and in 1992 —at the time of his abrupt disappearance—he was working as a trapeze artist at the Southern Cross Circus, a local establishment based just a few miles from here. The circus closed for good the night he disappeared. I have no idea if he was connected to anything, but on the same night he disappeared, a co-performer's act was sabotaged, and two elderly ladies in a neighboring care home were smothered in their beds.'

Steve leaned back in the chair and whistled through his teeth.

'Well, I'll be damned. I always knew he was an asshole, but it seems like he took it to a higher level than I ever imagined.'

21

DESPITE A LINGERING BRUISE reminding Slim of how they had met, Steve was keen to stay involved in the investigation and told Slim to get in touch whenever he needed anything. He was also keen to meet the grandparents he had never known existed, so Slim made another call to Don, requesting an address and contact details for Jason's family. He asked Steve to hold off for a while until he had investigated Jason's involvement in events a little further, but he felt certain he would need to speak to them himself at some point, too.

It was time, though, to close the initial part of his investigation.

Maria was waiting in the service area café off the M5 outside Worcester. At eleven in the morning it was busy but not crowded, and she had found a table by the window surrounded by several other empty tables. Her walking stick leaned against the window glass and she was reading a paperback crisp enough to suggest it had just been bought.

'I have to say, you pick the most romantic of locations,'

she said with a wry smile as he sat down. 'And your punctuality is second to none. If I drink any more coffee they're liable to run out.'

'I'm sorry,' Slim said, unable to raise himself to firing witticisms back. 'I got caught up.'

'So, what's this about?'

It was best to get straight to the point. 'I found him,' Slim said.

Maria let out a little gasp. 'Jason?'

'Yes.' He took a folder out of his bag and showed Maria the contents piece by piece. In addition to what Don had sent, he had some other pictures Steve had given him. As Maria looked them over, one hand covering her mouth, Slim talked through what he had found.

'It's likely he was guilty of something,' Slim said, as Maria wiped away a tear. 'I'm just not sure what.'

'At least it's closure of a sort,' Maria said. 'Although I'll never be able to look him in the eye and ask whether he frayed that rope.'

'How do you feel about things?'

Maria shrugged. 'Better than I'd expected to. I mean, whatever love for him I once had was long gone. We were only together briefly, and if what you told me his son said was true, I dodged a bullet. That doesn't mean there isn't a part of me still pining for the fantasy, though.'

'I'm glad to have helped, but sorry at the same time.'

There was an uncomfortable silence for a few seconds, then Maria said, 'You could walk away now, Slim. You found Jason. You could leave it there.'

'I know.'

'You're not going to, though, are you?'

He had given it a lot of thought during the drive down from Birmingham, and Maria was right. He could no more walk away now than declare his alcohol problems over. He was in too deep, and he needed to see the investigation through to its end.

He cleared his throat. 'Could you tell me everything you remember in the aftermath of your fall?'

Maria groaned and gave a tired laugh. 'You know, I've never met anyone quite like you, Slim.'

22

I<small>T WAS</small> a surprise that Jane Cornick would accept his booking, but two weeks after abruptly leaving, Slim found himself checking in to the little B&B in the centre of Meadow Cross, this time under his own name.

'I thought I'd recognised you the first time,' Jane Cornick said, as she handed over the keys to the same room as before. 'I do love a good crime documentary. Did you know it was that arrogant so-and-so all along?'

'Ah, which arrogant so-and-so are you referring to?'

'Oh, I'd have to look it up. A bit like a spy thriller, isn't it? Do you often travel under different names?'

Slim tugged at the collar of his coat, the room suddenly feeling oppressively hot. 'Ah, from time to time. I apologise for not being straight with you before.'

'It's all right. As long as you pay up and no one's banging on the door at midnight, I don't mind. Although it would liven things up around here a bit. It's all terribly dull, these days. So little worth gossiping about.' She chuckled. 'People are too busy staring at little screens to create any sort of scandal. By the way, did you ever get hold of Vanessa? I could have just given you her number, but you're a detective, aren't you?'

Certain now that Jane Cornick's niece was a dead end, Slim just shrugged. 'She hasn't returned my calls.'

'I'll give her a bell, tell her to pull her socks up. By the way, you're not single, are you? Needs a decent man, does our Vanessa. That last man she was with—Fred, I think his name was—he was a fiend.'

Slim said nothing, aware he had possibly seen the aftermath of Fred's handiwork.

'Well, enjoy your stay,' Jane said. 'Let me know if you need anything.'

Slim smiled. 'Thank you.'

'And don't worry, if anyone does come knocking at midnight, I won't answer the door. My hearing's not what it once was.'

As April leaned towards May, bringing warmer weather, Slim downgraded his winter coat to a lighter jacket, and also shaved off most of his beard, but even so, as he walked through the village, allocating a little time to climb up to the top of the Cloverdale Hills, he felt like eyes were everywhere, watching him with suspicion. He had lost his anonymity through a slip of the tongue, exposing himself as a fraud at the same time. He came with baggage now, to anyone he encountered, but perhaps he could use that to his advantage.

He had learned during his time in the Iraqi desert, and over the subsequent years as a private investigator, that there were several ways to get people to talk. The easiest was to befriend them, be taken into their confidence. Tripping them up, making them say more than they meant, was another. Then there was the old favourite: to apply a little pressure. A private investigator had none of the power a police officer had, but there were many people who didn't know the difference.

Even so, solving a thirty-year-old mystery was never going to be easy. He had pushed himself out of his comfort zone and set up a couple of social media pages requesting information and possible photographs from the last few performances of Southern Cross Circus, but so far had received no interesting responses. He had also sent an email to the local television station that had run the short video segment but had not yet received a response to that either.

He was sitting on a bench, sipping from a flask of coffee and enjoying the view when he heard a chuckle from behind him. He looked around and found Katie Julius standing there, wearing her familiar power-walking gear.

'Well, if it isn't the most Googled man in Meadow Cross. I admit, I did have a look myself. It's almost an honour to have you poking around in our bushes. Perhaps they'll consider erecting a statue.'

Slim smiled. 'Hopefully a stone one and not one made out of straw.'

Katie laughed. 'Don't worry. It rains too much around here for anything to catch alight. So, have you figured it all out yet?'

Slim shook his head. 'No.'

'Perhaps there's nothing much to uncover after all. And it was a long time ago. Things get buried, don't they?'

Slim nodded. 'And so do people.'

Katie came and sat beside him on the bench. 'You really think those two old ladies were murdered?'

'I'm certain of it. I even have a good suspect. What I don't have is a motive, nor any proof.'

'How are you going to get it?'

Slim shrugged. 'I have no idea.'

'I thought you were a private detective?'

'I am. But proving wild guesses isn't that easy.' He turned to look at her. Then, echoing her words to him on their first meeting, he smiled and said, 'From one outsider to another, what do you think happened?'

Katie wrinkled her mouth, then hummed under her breath. 'I don't really know the circumstances because I wasn't around then, and all I've heard is a few pub rumours, but don't you find it strange that someone would have killed two old women? I mean, it's doubling your chance of getting caught. And why kill them in the first place? That's a hate crime, isn't it? You hear these stories about people breaking into care homes and knocking off the patients in some cult-like protest at overpopulation, but in that case, why stop at two?'

'They got disturbed?'

'Maybe, but there was never a murder investigation, was there? The murder part was only ever a rumour. Officially both those ladies died of natural causes. It just so happened that they both died on the same night as that circus's final performance.'

'It's quite a coincidence, isn't it?'

'And you know who'll have the answers, don't you? Him who runs it. David Bellingham. Or failing him, his brother, Robert, who lives in the cottage next door.'

'I've met him. Walks with a limp? I was wandering about down there and he shooed me away.'

'A bit of a character, there. He has terminal cancer, although he's had it as long as I've been here. Plenty of rumours about him, too.'

'Such as?'

'This is just gossip, because I'm almost as big an outsider as you are, but there's quite a rivalry going on down there. Margaret, she was losing her marbles, so signed over assets to the boys while she was still alive. The favoured brother got the house, the other got the land in back. And when one brother expanded and improved a successful business, the other brother attempted to sabotage it.'

'How?'

Kate chuckled. 'Come on, use your imagination. How do you think?'

'By leasing the land to a circus?'

'Bingo.'

23

A YOUNG RECEPTIONIST showed him to a seat, then went back into her office and picked up the phone. While he waited, Slim peered down the corridor into Oak House. It seemed like a nice place, well lit and airy, without that musty blanket smell Slim associated with care homes. Nice pictures hung on the wall, and pleasant background music played faintly. He saw a couple of patients cross the corridor on walking frames and even heard laughter. He had never known his father but had his mother still been alive, he would never have wasted his money putting her in a decent place like this.

He was still musing on unsettling memories when a tall man nearly old enough to be a patient approached, lifting a hand to acknowledge him.

'Mr. Hardy?' David said with a cheerful smile, seemingly unaware of Slim's newfound local infamy. 'Welcome to Oak House. Please follow me.'

The little office room at the far end of the corridor was perfect, even more so when Bellingham went to sit behind a wide IKEA desk, leaving Slim to take a seat by the door.

The care home owner shuffled about to get comfortable, adjusting the light sweater he wore over a dress shirt and tie. He started to cross one leg over the other, appeared to think better of it, then leaned forward instead, steepling his hands on the desk.

'I'd like to thank you for your interest in Oak House,' he said. 'It's an honour to have you choose our small, family-run business for your aunt.'

'My aunt … yes, that's right,' Slim said. 'I read your brochure. You do a lot to make your residents comfortable.'

'End of life does not mean end of care,' Bellingham said, directly quoting from the company website. He went on for a while, unloading buzzword spiel which Slim soaked up, waiting for anything that might help him.

'Your aunt is eighty-eight, I believe?' Bellingham said at last. 'And she has trouble walking?'

Slim tried to remember what he'd written on the contact form, and wished he'd saved a copy of the information before sending it. 'That's correct,' he said.

'We have a few vacant rooms on the ground floor,' Bellingham said.

'Her eyesight is still excellent,' Slim said. 'She'd prefer a room with a view. Ideally of those hills to the northeast, rather than that patch of waste ground out the back. Didn't there used to be a circus out there?'

Slim wondered if he'd dropped the hint a little too early, but Bellingham just shrugged. 'A long time ago,' he said with a hint of bitterness, looking down at the desktop. Then, looking up at Slim, he said, 'Regrettably—if you get my meaning—we might have an upstairs vacancy within the next few weeks. Shall we go and have a look?'

Slim was happy to trail Bellingham around the halls of Oak House, asking as many questions as he could think of in order to stretch out the tour for as long as possible. He was yet to discover which rooms had been used by Margaret and Carrie on the night both had died, but he was trying to ascertain how a potential killer might have entered the building. However, noticing the telltale signs of renovation work, he was only too aware that the house's layout might have changed over the last thirty years.

'You have adequate security?' he asked, trying to sound like a concerned nephew.

'CCTV and alarms on all the doors,' Bellingham said.

'And the windows?'

'The ground floor windows are alarmed. The upper floors are not, but I don't think you need to worry.'

'And the system is maintained regularly?'

'It's checked on a yearly basis,' Bellingham said, glancing at Slim with a look of suspicion that made Slim wonder if he was pushing it too far. 'I can assure you that your aunt will be quite safe.'

Afraid of blowing his cover, Slim opted to change the subject, instead questioning Bellingham on the meal service and adherence to dietary requirements as they walked along an upper floor corridor and down a flight of rear stairs which passed a fire door leading out into the courtyard. It was a good place to gain entry, Slim noted. However, from differences in the shade of the wallpaper and the coving around the ceiling, Slim felt certain the door was part of a more recent renovation.

As they arrived back in the downstairs lobby, Bellingham crossed his hands over his stomach. 'Thank you for coming, Mr. Hardy, and do be in touch if you think our establishment will be suitable for your aunt.'

'I appreciate your time,' Slim said. 'Thanks again.'

As he went outside, he felt a sense of oppression lifting off his shoulders. He stood on the path outside the main doors for a while, looking out across the gardens. Then, as he started off, he glanced back over his shoulder, and saw David Bellingham standing just inside the door, a grim expression on his face and a mobile phone pressed against his ear.

24

Slim called Vanessa on the way back to the B&B, but yet again got no answer. Frustrated, he thought about calling Don for an update, but changed his mind. Don would call when something came up.

He hadn't eaten since that morning so went into the shop to buy a sandwich. Feeling a little nervous about his reception, he was pleased to find Jessica's son working behind the counter instead of his mother, alongside a pretty but sullen teenage girl. As Slim walked down the single aisle, picking out a sandwich and a chocolate bar, he heard an exaggerated whisper from the boy to the girl.

'That's him! That guy I told you about.'

'Shh!'

Slim smiled inwardly to himself, forced himself to show no reaction, and pretended to look through a football magazine for a couple of minutes. The whispers continued, but the volume was too low for him to make out what was being said.

At last, certain their curiosity was embedded and wondering how to work it to his advantage, Slim approached the counter. He set the sandwich and chocolate bar down, then pointed to a customer coffee machine on the counter.

'And I'll have a double espresso,' he said, aware that the time gained to encourage a conversation would be worth the poor quality of the drink.

The boy got to work, while the girl, seemingly here just to hang out, watched him with interest through eyes heavily outlined with black eyeliner, although he felt she would have been prettier without it.

The boy set the coffee down and mumbled a price Slim could barely hear. As he paid, then gathered his purchases, the girl clearly wasn't going to let him just leave.

'You're that detective guy, aren't you? The one with the pretend name?'

'Helen, shut up!'

Slim turned, gave them both a long glance, then smiled. 'That's right,' he said. 'My name's John Hardy, although most people call me Slim. You can choose.'

'Slim?'

'Helen…!'

Slim smiled at the boy. 'It's all right. What should I call you?'

'Dez,' Helen said before the boy could answer. 'It's short for Derek, lol.'

The way she actually said "lol" as a word made Slim smile. He looked at Derek, who was squirming, head tucked against his shoulder in embarrassment.

'Derek is a fine name,' Slim said. 'But if you don't like it, you can just make up another one, like I did.'

'Why?' Helen said.

Slim chuckled. 'Because I wanted to ask questions that people might not have answered if they knew who I really was.'

'Isn't that fraud?'

'He's a policeman,' Derek said. 'He can do what he likes.'

'I'm a private detective,' he said.

'Like Sherlock Holmes,' Helen said to Derek.

'But not as good,' Slim said. 'I have a tendency to make stupid mistakes, like revealing my real name to a church full of people.'

'What are you investigating?' Helen said.

'A friend of mine used to work in the circus that was once found behind the Oak House care home, on the road to Belbroughton. She was in an accident she believes was caused by deliberate sabotage. On the same night, her boyfriend—another performer—disappeared without trace. I decided to investigate it for her.'

'Did you find him?'

Slim nodded. He had to quietly admit that he enjoyed the twin looks of surprise.

'I did,' he said. 'He's dead now, but he actually changed his name and moved to America.'

'So you figured it out?' Helen said. 'That's pretty cool.'

'If you found him, why are you still here?' Derek asked.

'Because I want to know why he disappeared,' Slim said. 'And currently I don't have a clue.'

'Because it was him who did the sabotage?'

Slim shrugged. 'Maybe. Then why do it in the first place?'

'Perhaps he wanted someone else to get the blame,' Derek said.

'Also possible,' Slim said. 'What I'd really like to know is who was there that night, the night of the last performance, when the accident happened.'

'Don't you have any photos?'

Slim shook his head. 'Nothing. I thought there might

be some old newspaper articles, but I haven't been able to find anything. It looks like they were removed from the library's microfiche catalogue.'

'Spooky,' Helen said.

'Quite.' Slim glanced at the clock on the wall behind the counter. 'Well, I'd better be off. If you hear any decent rumours, come and find me over at the B&B.'

They both nodded wordlessly, regarding him as though he were some kind of bandit about to make off with the spoils of a heist.

He went back to the B&B, ate his food, then took a shower. He still didn't feel like he was getting very far, but he lay down on the bed anyway and opened his laptop, hoping for some nugget of new information to raise a hand and reveal itself. The social media groups he had set up were still empty besides a few spammers he wasted time trying to find out how to delete, and he'd had no emails. He browsed the web instead for a while, looking for something he might have missed. In the end, he got up and headed downstairs, too wired to sleep.

It was still light outside, so he walked up the road, past Katie Julius's place to St Steven's church. The main door was locked so he wandered through the graveyard, taking a look at some of the inscriptions, noting the ages of the deceased, from someone who had lived to 104, to another dead at two months. It was a lottery, he thought sometimes, and at fifty he had probably outstayed his welcome.

A cool wind was blowing down from the Cloverdale Hills, so he wandered over to the church's rear door, wondering if he could get inside that way. He was nearly there though when he heard the clack of something hard tapping on the flagstones of the path.

Instinctively he ducked out of sight inside the little porch. Peering around the wall, he watched a stooped figure with a walking stick make its way off the path and over to the graves in the furthest corner.

Slim might have dismissed the figure as a common mourner were it not for the clutch of red flowers in one hand.

A few feet from Margaret Bellingham's grave, the figure leaned the stick against another flagstone and walked the last few steps unaided. They then bent down, replaced the dead flowers in the pot with the ones he had brought, then stood back up, said a few words Slim couldn't hear, and turned to leave.

As the figure walked back to where they had left the stick, Slim got a clear look at the person beneath the hood of a light wind-cheater.

Robert Bellingham.

25

SLIM WAS WOKEN by the buzzing of his phone, a moment before it fell off his bedside table and crashed to the floor. Rather surprisingly for his Nokia, the battery cover had popped off, and it took him a moment to reinsert the battery and restore power.

He had a missed call from Don, but when he returned the call he got no answer. Instead, he got up, made a coffee, then sat by the window of his room, gazing out at the glimmer of sunlight over the distant mound of the Cloverdale Hills, wondering about a thought he had had while lying in bed.

Someone in the village had a secret, he felt sure of it. It was time to start pulling up stones, rattling doors a little. If just one person would talk, it might give him the ammunition to draw a confession out of another.

After having breakfast downstairs, during which time he found out he was again the B&B's only customer, he asked Jane while she was tidying up what she knew of David and Robert Bellingham.

She frowned, adjusting her apron. 'Is this for your investigation?'

'It might be?'

Jane chuckled. 'How exciting. Well, I don't know either particularly well, I have to say. We went to the same school but they were a few years above me. I saw them about from time to time. David was … how can I say? The "smooth" one. Always had a girlfriend. That he never married was a surprise, but he probably couldn't make a choice. And Robert … he was a bit troubled. He was always fighting, didn't seem to know where he was going in life. I couldn't say they stood out that much from other kids, though.'

From estimating Jane's age, Slim surmised that she was talking about the late fifties or early sixties.

'What did they do after they left school? Did either do any time in the Armed Forces, the police, anything like that?'

He was looking for anything that might have hardened either boy from playground tearaways into possible criminals. Jane, however, just laughed.

'Not that I know of. I used to bump into Robert from time to time. He was working in Woolworths in Stourbridge for a while and I remember one day pushing the kids in the pram through the park and he was there cutting the hedges. He always seemed to have three jobs at once.'

'What about David?'

'Oh, I have no idea really. I never saw him around much. Once or twice in the shop or up in Stourbridge. We were never friends so never had much to say to each other beyond a polite hello or good afternoon.'

Slim gave a thoughtful nod. 'Do you know how long he's been running Oak House?'

'Oh, from the mid-eighties, I think. His parents ran it

for years but his father died a long time ago, and I think after his mother got sick, she had to give up the running of it and pass it on to David.'

'And she became a resident there?'

'I believe so. I'm sorry, I don't know what was wrong with her. I wasn't so big on idle gossip back in those days.' Jane chuckled. 'That comes with old age, I think.'

Jane had to excuse herself to get on with her daily chores, so after breakfast Slim went for a walk up to the church, hoping to bump into Reverend Thomas. Again, the church was locked, but as he looked at the graves of Margaret Bellingham and Carrie Thompson—one with fresh flowers, the other with none—another idea presented itself, so he found a bench and called another contact from his Armed Forces days. While they had never been close friends, Slim and Alan Coaker had a grudging respect for each other. Alan now ran a security firm in London and sounded as displeased as ever to hear Slim's voice.

'I got your cheque,' he said with a gruff chuckle. 'It just about covered your postage for 2018. I won't hold out for any more.'

'Little by little,' Slim said. 'I always pay my debts. Eventually.'

'What can I put on your account this time?' Alan said.

'I need some surveillance gear,' Slim said, then detailed what he required. Alan listened, promised to do what he could, then hung up, leaving Slim wondering what might show up, remembering the time he had asked Alan for something to pick a lock and had been sent a pair of bolt cutters.

After finishing the call, he rang Donald Lane back.

'Don, sorry I missed your call. What have you got for me?'

'All good, Slim. Listen to this. I told you I'd found a boarding pass for Lowery Powell on a flight to Malaga.'

'I remember.'

'Well, I got a copy of the landing card. I'll send it over. He lists his occupation as "entertainer" and his address as Oak House. Why would he do that? In any case, we can at least extend his paper trail and we know he got off the plane. I've been trying to find out what happened to him after that, but no luck so far.'

'Thanks, Don, that's great.'

'I'm still looking into some of the other things you mentioned. I'll be in touch soon.'

Don hung up. Slim stared at his phone for a moment, then got up and hurried back to the B&B to check his email.

He had just made it to the street corner outside the B&B when he heard a voice hail him from across the street.

'Hey, ah, Mr. Detective.'

He stopped and turned. Jessica's son, Derek, was standing outside the shop. As Slim waited, Derek checked for traffic then jogged across to where he stood.

'Hello again,' Slim said. 'Shouldn't you be in school?'

Derek rolled his eyes. 'It's Saturday.'

Slim chuckled. 'I should have known that. How can I help you?'

'I found some photos,' Derek said. 'Of that circus you were talking about. Mum and Dad went there. I found them in a box. There was something else, too. Like a tape thing.'

He reached into his pocket and pulled out a VHS tape. A faded label sticker said "Circus (date with Jess)" in scrawled handwriting. Slim stared at the date written underneath with nervous disbelief.

Sept. 26, '92.

'It's a video tape,' Slim said. 'I haven't seen one of those in a while. You play them on a video player.'

'We used to have one but it got thrown away a few years back. Mum doesn't play these anymore, not since Dad left.'

Slim looked down. 'I'm sorry, I had no idea.'

Derek shrugged. 'It's all right. He only lives in Hagley. I see him pretty often.'

'It can't be easy, though.'

'It's not too bad. Do you want these?'

'I'd love to take a look.'

'It was pretty hard to get them. If Mum finds out, she'll kill me.'

Slim resisted a smile. 'I'll give you twenty quid.'

Derek smiled, then sighed. 'I was hoping you could buy me a bottle of something. Like vodka, or brandy? I want to impress Helen, but they're so strict on I.D.s these days, and Mum's shop has cameras.'

Before joining the Armed Forces and having the soul ripped out of him by his experiences in Iraq, Slim had been a teenager, and had experienced the same tribulations he saw in Derek's eyes. For a moment he almost said yes, then gave a slow shake of his head.

'Take it from a man who's ruined plenty of relationships with drink,' he said. 'There are better ways to impress a girl. Buy her a book or something.' He smiled. 'Or a decent coffee machine.' He pulled out his wallet and took out three twenties. 'This should cover both.'

With his eyes lighting up, Derek took the money and pocketed it. 'Thanks,' he said, barely able to keep a smile off his face. He handed over the tape, before pulling an envelope from his pocket and hurriedly pushing it into Slim's hand.

'I appreciate it,' Slim said, putting the tape and the

envelope out of sight into his jacket pocket. 'And I consider it a loan. I'll give them back once I'm finished with them.' At Derek's worried look, he added, 'But you can keep the money. And good luck with the girl. She seems … interesting.'

Derek gave a shy nod, so Slim bid him goodbye and headed for the B&B. As he reached the door he glanced back and saw Derek standing where he had left him, watching Slim with a look of adulation on his face. Slim waved again, then headed inside, hoping he'd inspired the boy to end up like someone other than himself.

26

DON'S COPIES of Lowery Powell's boarding pass and landing card were both scanned, but even though the copies were poor quality, Slim could tell from the scrawled writing on the landing pass that Lowery had regarded it with the same tired irritation that Slim had on the few times he had flown. That they were even kept had come as a surprise; he would have thought the storage space would have been put to better use for something else.

Where had Powell gone after landing in Malaga? Had he planned to move on somewhere else, or was he still there, working incognito in a bar?

To his regret, Slim knew he might never find out. However, if he could at least establish what had made Powell close down the circus so abruptly and take off across Europe, he might at least close one door of the many in the investigation which still stood open.

The photos Derek had given him, while interesting, gave few insights into what had happened that night. Excited to know Jessica had been there at the final performance, the photos were rather sanitised, several shots of a young couple he assumed to be Jessica and her boyfriend—likely Derek's father—along with a few more of distant, vague circus acts. A trapeze artist was too blurry to make out; three clowns were distant blots of colour. A man breathing fire was a bright eruption of flame with a shadow underneath.

One, however, was striking. The young couple—and Slim found himself wearing a nostalgic smile at just how pretty Jessica had once been—had managed to get themselves a group photo with a large, grinning man in full ring master's regalia who dominated the photo, reducing Jessica and her boyfriend to mere side notes. He had bright green eyes, almost emerald, and his gaze was so intense Slim found it hard to look directly at the photograph. He wore a top hat made of what looked like purple felt, and a red jacket over a blue checked shirt buttoned up with a black bow tie. A black mustache curled up at the corners, topping a thin, knowing smile.

Slim stared at him for a long time. More than anything, he was struck by how young Powell looked. Even with his costume adding years, he could be no older than thirty.

Finding the photograph a little unsettling, he put it at the bottom of the pile and turned his attention to the VHS tape. He would need a video player, and after a brief check online discovered he could order one but it would take a few days to arrive, he decided to take a drive up to Hagley and Stourbridge and see if he could find one in a charity shop somewhere.

He had just turned off Kidderminster Road, heading for Hagley's small shopping centre, when he noticed a building that rang a tinkling bell at the back of his mind.

The Pig and Pen, a pub standing on a street corner just back from the main road. It was just after four in the afternoon, so the pub was probably open.

He pulled into to a space along the kerb a short distance from the pub and got out. As he stared at the building, the sign hanging off the wall creaking in the breeze, he took a deep breath.

He didn't have to drink, he knew that. But it made it easier to keep his sobriety by staying away from temptation.

Sometimes, though, the only way to appreciate the light was to enter the darkest of places. Clenching a fist around his car keys as a sign of resilience, Slim walked up to the entrance door, took another deep breath, and went inside.

The pub was bright and airy, modern, and lacking the kind of atmosphere that history brought. There was too much space between tables by the window and a long, right-angled bar for it to be cozy, but filled with people it would have been pleasant enough. As it was, the bar was empty, BBC Radio 2 playing at a low volume out of a speaker over the bar. Slim took a stool at the bar and waited.

'Be right there,' called a voice from through a doorway, and a moment later a large man appeared, carrying a box of crisps. He set it down on the bar, and looked up at Slim, his smile dropping.

Without his clerical robes, Gavin Thomas looked like a different person. He could have been ten years younger, but at the same time a no-nonsense look in his eyes, tattoos not quite concealed beneath shirt sleeves, and shoulders built by lifting beer barrels, labelled as a man not to be messed with. As Gavin's eyes reflected open hostility, Slim wondered if he'd made a grave mistake coming here.

'Hello again,' he said, clearly making a point of controlling the emotion in his voice. 'I thought you'd be long gone by now.'

'I apologise for what happened at the church,' Slim said. 'It's true what I said. I shouldn't be here.'

'Then why are you?'

'I'm a man with questions. And I think you might have some of the answers.'

'I've heard what you're asking about. No one round here wants to talk about that circus. It's gone, it's in the past. Let it go.'

'I don't want to let it go. I want to know what happened. I have a friend who nearly died that night. She fell when her trapeze rope broke, having been deliberately sabotaged. I think she would like to know who was responsible.'

Gavin's face softened a little. 'I don't know anything about that. I didn't see it. I don't know what happened.'

'But you were there that night, weren't you?'

Gavin's hands had clenched into fists. Slim saw scars on some knuckles, misshapen lumps on others. They were a map of fist fighting history, and Slim wondered whether his own face would soon join a list of those that had been pummeled. He had given and taken his share over the years, but while he could handle himself, Gavin Thomas was a different proposition, out of his league.

'I was there for a while, yes, but I wasn't there when the girl fell.'

'Where were you?'

Gavin looked ready to unleash a volley of thunder. 'I don't need to tell you anything.'

Slim leaned forward, feeling a sudden surge of adrenaline. 'But you want to, don't you? Come on, Gavin. Get it off your chest. It's been eating you up for years, hasn't it? Where were you when Maria fell?'

'I was up on the Cloverdale Hills.'

'Can you prove it?'

105

Gavin shook his head. 'No. The person I was with …
he disappeared.'

Slim felt a tremble pass through his gut. 'Who?'

'His name was Jason. He was one of the performers.'

Slim's hands felt suddenly cold, and he needed a drink
more than anything else in the world.

'What were you doing?'

Gavin's gaze never wavered, but he swallowed hard,
then sighed.

'I was having a word with him.'

27

TO BE FAIR TO GAVIN, as he had gone behind the bar and poured himself a large brandy, he had refused Slim's attempt to join him, and now Slim sat, a coffee in front of him, staring at the glass of amber liquid while trying to focus on the words of the former career criminal turned man of the cloth.

'Us local kids, we hated them. You'd see them about the village, and they just looked like freaks. That's what we told ourselves, anyway. Gypo scum, we used to call them. I was still a kid when that circus showed up, already going off the rails, one of those angry tough types who needed a sense of place. I needed somewhere to rule. Do you know what I mean?'

Slim gave a slow nod, fixing his gaze on Gavin's face and trying to forget about the drink he could smell, could almost taste.

'You ... needed to be top dog,' he said, 'but you weren't.'

'We had a local crew,' Gavin said. 'Me, Sev, Deano, Ballsy, Tone, a couple of others on the fringes who'd hang from time to time. We weren't bad kids but from Hagley down to Belbroughton we were the main guys. Sev went off to university and even though I was younger than Ballsy and Tone, I was our next natural leader. Only by then we'd started to have run ins with these circus guys.'

'They were on your turf, so to speak?'

Gavin gave a wistful smile. 'It sounds ridiculous, doesn't it? But for a bunch of hardnut teenagers, it was everything. Suddenly you've got men in tights wandering about, loudmouths with weird accents, really tall people, really short people, and we just couldn't get used to it. We never did anything other than a bit of harassment, though. We'd shout insults at them from the car, that kind of thing.' He sighed, tapping a finger on the glass. 'And then Jason showed up, and starting crossing a line.'

'What line?'

'He was good-looking, muscular, cool, exotic. And the local girls just fell into his arms. He was pulling them all over the place, and that got under our skin like nothing else. He wasn't the only one trying to pick up the local girls, but he was the only one who was shameless about it. He was like a kid in a sweet shop, and everyone knew. And then he went one step even further, and started playing around with my girlfriend.'

Slim whistled through his teeth. 'I take it that didn't go down well.'

'Elaine Baxter, she lived up in Hagley but she was working weekends in the Spar, which is where he met her, I suppose. He got her pregnant. I know it was him, because she wasn't putting out for me. She'd been playing around with him behind my back for several months. She broke down that afternoon and told me. I got a couple of guys together and we went down there to have a word.'

'And by have a word, you don't mean have a word.'

Gavin shook his head. He let out a long sigh and drained what was left of his brandy. Seeing it disappear gave Slim hope he could survive the pub without losing his mind.

'Deano, he lived down Meadow Cross Lane and had just got his first car, so he drove. Tone, Ballsy and me grabbed Jason and threw him in the car. We took him up to the Cloverdale Hills, down the forest trail where cars aren't supposed to go. We'd roughed him up already so I knew I could handle it, so I told the boys to go back. After they were gone, I took Jason on down the track.' Gavin closed his eyes. 'I had a word with him.'

'And you left him there?'

Gavin's fingers had begun to tremble. 'He was still breathing, but I … I was scared I'd gone too far.' He rubbed his eyes. 'I had … no control in those days. You know people talk about a red mist….' He shook his head. 'I bolted, going back down to the circus, trying to pretend I'd never left. Deano had met up with his girlfriend, so I don't know what he told her, but by the time I made it there were ambulances down there. It put the fear of God in me, but it had nothing to do with Jason. It was the girl who had fallen off the trapeze.'

28

SLIM HAD WANTED to know more while Gavin was in such a confessional mood, but a group of regular customers had arrived, drawing Gavin's attention. He had told Slim to stop by the pub or the church if he wanted to know anything else, but said there was little he could add. The circus had closed that night after the furore surrounding the trapeze accident, never to reopen. Within a couple of days the performers had all gone, and within two weeks everything left behind had been bulldozed or removed.

And in regards to Jason Felton, the police had never come knocking.

Slim had asked one last question, about the other people who had taken Jason up to the Cloverdale Hills.

'Ballsy's long gone. Car crash back in the nineties. He was only twenty-two, but he was a maniac. No one was surprised. Tone moved down to London years ago. Deano —Kevin Dean—he lives in Hagley. He got married but they divorced a few years after. He straightened up years before I did. We don't see each other these days but last I heard he was doing good, working in some company.'

'What about Elaine Baxter? Your girlfriend?'

Gavin looked down. For a moment his fingers drummed harder than ever. 'She didn't make it,' he said quietly. 'Neither of them made it. And I think that pushed me down the spiral for a while. Even now … I pray for them every day.' He looked up, tears in his eyes. 'I'd better get over to these guys. It was nice to talk to you, Slim.' He smiled. 'It was … cathartic.'

Slim went out, into the late evening sunlight. For a while he just leaned back against the pub wall, hands pressed against the cold pebbledash, embarrassed to admit that he was almost as overawed by his ability to survive being inside the pub as he was by the gravity of Gavin's confession.

The picture was slowly becoming clearer, but so much was based on trusting the word of people who were there. He now had a clearer idea of what had happened to Jason, but still the fates of the two old women eluded him. Maybe they really were unconnected, a simple matter of coincidence.

Somehow, however, Slim found that unlikely.

He was exhausted down to his bones, so he headed back to the B&B. The Spar was closed, so he drove up to the Nepalese restaurant outside St Steven's and got some takeaway, which he ate in his room. Then, with it getting dark outside, he lay on his bed and attempted to sleep.

It wasn't likely. Too many ideas were swirling around inside his head. Firstly, he needed to corroborate Gavin's story. He needed to speak to both Jessica at the Spar and her ex-husband, to see if there was anything they had seen that night to confirm the timeline that Gavin had suggested. And what if Gavin had spun him the tale just to cover some other misdemeanour? While Slim wanted to believe the words of the former criminal turned to the church—and his words had been thoroughly convincing—it was a common method for a guilty party to "over-talk", hamming up some minor crime in order to mask involvement in a greater one. While Gavin was unlikely to be charged for a historical assault on a man now deceased, had he also been involved in the deaths of either woman, or indeed the sabotage of Maria's trapeze, he could yet face more serious charges.

Jason's death too made it hard to prove whether the assault had ever taken place. Slim planned to ask Steve if there had been any scars on his father's face which might have given an indication of a prior assault, but he knew well from his own experience that not all beatings left scars.

Eventually sleep must have found him because he woke up in the pre-dawn, still groggy and half dressed from the night before, his head feeling muggy and almost hungover from a succession of bad dreams. He got up, pulled himself together with a hot shower and a strong coffee, then sat at his desk, staring at notes scrawled on sheets of crumpled paper, trying to make sense of things.

To his surprise, when he opened his computer he found an email from an archivist at the local television news station. The woman thanked him for his message, told him that she had managed to find the local news segment he had requested, and that while for copyright reasons she couldn't send him a copy, he was quite welcome to visit a local storage facility to view it at his leisure. With an unexpected smile at such a stroke of luck, Slim sent a message back, requesting an appointment later that afternoon.

With a purpose to his day now established, Slim had a

bounce in his step as he headed downstairs for breakfast. Even more so when Jane Cornick came over to his table carrying a large box.

'A courier delivery for you this morning,' she told him, handing over the box, which was light for its size. It had a sender's address in London, so after breakfast Slim took it out to his car, drove a little way out of the village to a quiet layby and then opened it in private.

Alan Coaker, unsurprisingly, had disguised a rather tiny device with an excessive amount of packaging, although otherwise hadn't played any familiar tricks. There was a birthday card in the bottom, the envelope unsealed, with a simple message which said: "I don't know when it is, but I took the cost of your present off your outstanding bill. It wasn't much. Cheers, Alan".

Slim gave a wry smile at Coaker's attempt at wit, but in fairness the device was exactly what he wanted: a voice recorder triggered by human utterances, and suitable for outdoor weather. Figuring there was no better time than the present, particularly because it was still earlier than most people would be up and about, he turned the car around, headed back to the village, and placed the recorder in his desired position before his presence could be noted or cause suspicion. Then, he headed for Stourbridge.

The only electrical store in town had no video players for sale, so Slim found himself wandering from one charity shop to the next, hoping to find what he wanted. Most, however, perhaps overawed by the amount of junk they invariably received, had none. One shop assistant told him they occasionally had such items donated, but they just took up valuable shelf space, so were usually taken to the local tip. The man, however, suggested he try a local covered arcade which had a bric-a-brac market.

There, finally, amidst heaps of jumbled old appliances, the shop's elderly owner helped him find a dusty video player he claimed was in working order. The price was practically nothing, so Slim gave the man a twenty and told him to keep the change.

Even though Slim wanted to get back on the road, the man was keen to write out a receipt, in case Slim found the machine didn't work after all and wanted to return it. While he waited, he looked over the piles of junk heaped behind the counter and had a sudden thought.

'How long have you been here?' he asked, as the man passed across the receipt, which Slim put into his pocket.

'Me or the shop, lad?'

'The shop.'

The man scratched his head. 'Must be going on forty years.'

'There used to be a circus down in Meadow Cross,' Slim said. 'I don't suppose you'd have anything relating to that? Memorabilia, that kind of thing.'

'Huh. You's the first one who's ever asked about that place. Might have something out the back. I make it a rule to never throw nothin' away. Hang on a sec, I'll have a look.'

He shuffled out through a door barely visible between piles of assorted books, magazines, chairs, tables, stools, old toasters, and a million other things. As Slim listened to the old man shuffling about for some minutes, he wondered if he had become lost, never to return. Then, just as he was about to give up hope, the old man reappeared, carrying a tatty shoebox in his arms.

'I don't have much but this is what I've got,' he said, setting the box down on the countertop and removing the lid, which had long ago been ripped nearly in half and repaired by a thick piece of now yellowing tape. 'There's not much here. A few programmes and whatnot. A few nicknacks. It's all yours if you want it.'

'Thank you very much,' Slim said.

He had some time to kill before his appointment at the television archive facility, so he found a café, ordered a drink, and sat down at a corner table, where he went through the box of memorabilia. Mostly it contained a series of programmes and old tickets dated between 1988 and 1991. The programmes were of most interest, with a detailed editorial about circus history, followed by profiles of each performer. Afterwards, there were performance times, followed by schedules for future performances, tours, and then a page of discount coupons that could be cut out.

The profiles were of the most interest to Slim. Each performer had a picture with a brief bio alongside. From The Extraordinary Edgar the Firebreather to Calamity the Clown and his Clumsy Companions, many sounded delightfully fantastical. Others were more mundane, from Frank Leworski the tightrope walker to Gordon Smith the contortionist.

One thing Slim noticed was the high turnover of staff. From the earliest programme dated Spring 1989, only three performers remained in the most recent, from Summer 1991. Neither Jason nor Maria featured at all, having both joined the staff late in the circus's existence, and the only other constant was the face on the inside cover, that of a grinning, top hat-wearing Lowery Powell. Unlike the other performers, with those who had remained having updated pictures in each edition, Powell's picture was the same, except for one edition where it had been partially obscured by an extravagant signature and a message in flowing script it took Slim a few minutes to decode as saying, "Dear Matthew, I hope you enjoy the show!"

Who Matthew was, Slim might never know, but as he stared at Lowery Powell's message, he thought of something he ought to check if he could find time.

It was time to go, however, so Slim packed away the box, finished his coffee, and headed for his car.

It was only a ten-minute drive across town to the television station archive facility. It was far smaller than Slim had expected. The image in his head had been of a large, grey warehouse on an industrial estate, but instead he found himself standing outside a three-storey building in the middle of a line of terraced houses.

He pressed a buzzer and was let in to a cramped reception room. A grey-haired woman appeared, listened to his explanation, then nodded.

'Mr. Hardy, wasn't it? It was me who emailed you. I'm Carla Stapleton. Come this way, please.'

She led him down a narrow corridor to a little room where a flatscreen TV fitted onto the wall was connected to several ancient video recorders on the table in front of it. Carla showed Slim to a seat then took a video cassette out of a Ziplock bag.

'We're in the process of transferring everything to a digital archive, but it's only me and a couple of temps working on it, so it's taking a while. We haven't transferred this tape yet so if you don't mind, I can't let you touch it. They're not in great condition, and neither are our players.' She chuckled. 'Ancient technology.'

'That's fine,' Slim said.

'You wanted to watch a special news section about the Southern Cross Circus, which aired on June 21st, 1992?'

'That's right,' Slim said.

'I put the tape to the right place,' Carla said, then slid the tape into the machine.

Slim stared in fascination as the screen filled with a

grainy picture of a green and red circus big top. As the camera panned, it took in a line of stalls, a bouncy castle, and even a small Ferris Wheel.

'Southern Cross Circus,' came a voiceover. 'A local lucky charm, or a curse?'

The view switched to a tall man in a top hat. He was holding a cane under one arm, and twirling two tennis balls in the fingers of the other.

'Lowery Powell, owner and ring master, believes it to be the former.'

The shot changed to a closeup of Powell. 'We're a small operation,' he said, with a humility Slim found surprising. 'Our stand has only a capacity for two hundred people. I like to think of us as an introductory circus experience, one both for the fans and the performers. For many children it's their first circus experience. And for many performers, it's a place to learn their trade before moving on to bigger and better things.'

The camera cut to a line of people waiting to meet a group of performers who appeared to be signing autographs. It zoomed in on a young man and woman, both wearing sequinned bodysuits. As they turned to the camera, Slim realised with a start that he was looking at Jason and Maria. Jason was all Dan Dare jutting jaw and muscles, while Maria had a Grace Kelly coolness and confidence as she stared unflinching at the camera. Slim grimaced as he remembered Maria and the later pictures of Jason. Time could be cruel.

The assembled people appeared to be fans, and cheered as the camera panned across them. One held up a signed photograph.

'Is it true you're paid below minimum wage?' the voiceover said suddenly, shattering the aura of cool as both Jason and Maria looked at each other, their smiles replaced by shock. 'And are you aware that multiple health and safety regulations are being flaunted?'

'We're paid well,' Jason said, as Maria clutched against him like the 1950s film heroine she resembled. 'And all our equipment is quite safe.'

The scene cut to a group of dour locals standing on what Slim recognised as Meadow Cross Lane.

'They don't have adequate parking,' one man said, as a car whistling past almost obscured his voice. 'They're backed right up the lane here on a Friday. Can't get agricultural vehicles through.'

'Some clothes went missing off my line,' a woman said. 'I bet it was those damn gy—'

The camera cut again, this time to the inside of a shop. Slim couldn't help but smile at the poor quality of the video editing as the picture twisted and straightened. It zoomed in on a sign on the open door:

NO CIRCUS STAFF OR PERFORMERS.

'I had no choice,' an old woman was saying. 'They strip the paint off the shelves.'

The shot cut back to Lowery Powell, a continuation of his previous interview.

'Of course, some people will be suspicious of us. A circus carries that air of mystery, doesn't it? But prejudice can have hands and legs as well as a voice. My performers are classically trained, college educated. We've been accused of vandalism, theft. Who's to say it's not a consortium of locals, trying to ruin us?'

The shot cut to one of a group of performers warming up inside the big top, and a voiceover intoned, 'Love it or hate it, one thing you can say about the Southern Cross Circus is that opinion on it can be as spectacular as some of its acts.'

The segment cut to an advert and Carla leaned forward to switch off the tape.

'Would you like to see it again?' she asked.

Slim had Carla play the tape two more times before he began to feel he was outstaying his welcome, but nothing significant jumped out at him. Slim thanked Carla, then left. Sitting in his car, fingers drumming on the wheel, he tried to make sense of the effect the tape had had on him. Seeing Lowery Powell, Jason and Maria on screen, it made everything seem more real.

He was still staring straight ahead, out at the car park, where it had started to rain, when his phone buzzed in his pocket. Pulling it out, he pressed it to his ear before looking at the caller ID, expecting to hear Don's voice beginning another update. Instead, the other end of the line was fuzzy, as though the caller were using an old payphone.

'Mr. Hardy?' came a quiet voice Slim didn't recognise. 'Is it okay to talk to you now? I'm sorry I didn't get back to you before, but I was … scared.'

'Excuse me, but who is this?'

There was a long pause. Then, just as Slim was expecting the line to go dead, a quiet voice said, 'It's Vanessa.'

29

SLIM DROVE STRAIGHT TO BIRMINGHAM. Vanessa didn't want to meet him in public, so Slim picked her up at the end of an agreed street and they drove around the city, Slim choosing his route at random while Vanessa sat beside him, hunched up in the passenger seat as though afraid of being recognised.

For a long time she said nothing, just stared out of the passenger side window, the hood of her tracksuit top pulled up to her hairline. He studied her when he could, at junctions, when she lifted her head as they passed some landmark. Her face wore the scars of a hard life, but beneath the outer facade he could tell she was younger than he, made older by hair prematurely greying. She smelled of smoke and twice lit a cigarette, politely rolling down the window a little. She was gaunt, underfed. He couldn't tell if she drank or did drugs, but liked to think that holding down a job meant not. And there was no ring on her finger, but a reddish scar where one had been. Slim didn't like to think how hard it might have been wrenched off to break the skin.

'I'm nearly six months dry,' he said at last, when he could bear the silence no longer. 'The fear of starting again haunts me every day. What's haunting you?'

'The nightmares,' Vanessa said quietly.

'You worked at Oak House, didn't you?'

Instead of answering, Vanessa started to cry. She fumbled in her bag for another cigarette, but dropped it on the floor. As she scrabbled to reach it, her bag fell open, scattering its contents across Slim's lap. As Vanessa swore and tried to recover them, Slim saw a number of pill bottles, a tube of concealer, chewing gum. As Vanessa, gasping, sat upright, Slim smiled.

'It's all right. Sometimes I can't sleep either. And I get headaches too. Those aren't from the chemists, though, aren't they? You should see a doctor. He could prescribe something stronger. I can go with you if you like.'

'You don't even know me.'

'No, but I know plenty of people like you. Tell me about Oak House.'

Vanessa sniffed. Slim pulled a tissue out of a crumpled box squeezed into his door's side pocket and handed it to her. She wiped her nose then crumpled it and stuffed it into her hoodie's front pocket.

'I started there on work experience that summer,' she said. 'I was only fifteen. I made beds and chatted to old ladies for two weeks. Then, at the beginning of September I got a phone call from David Bellingham, the owner. Someone had quit and they were short-staffed. He offered me cash in hand to stay over a couple of nights a week, usually Friday and Saturday.'

'You were still at school?'

'Yeah, but he offered three fifty an hour.' Vanessa gave a sad chuckle. 'It was a fortune in those days.'

'Just nights?'

'I started at seven, did general chores until ten or so, then basically watched TV or dozed in a chair. If one of the residents needed anything, they would pull a cord by their bed that rang a bell. Every two hours I had to do a circuit of the corridors, so I'd set an alarm clock, get up and wander round, then go back to sleep.'

'You were alone?'

Vanessa nodded. 'David had a room downstairs where he slept. I was supposed to call him if there was any trouble.'

'And was there?'

Vanessa started crying again. Slim reached for another tissue, then thought better of it and pulled the whole box free and handed it across.

'Only on that night, but I didn't know it at the time.'

'Why? What happened? What did you see?'

'A man,' Vanessa said quietly. 'A man coming out of one of the resident's rooms. He … he—' Her voice was trembling so badly she could barely speak. 'He … wasn't supposed to be in there.'

Slim pulled the car into a supermarket car park and stopped by the kerb. With Vanessa sobbing in the passenger seat, he pulled a file of assorted photographs out of his bag.

'Did you recognise him?' he asked.

'No—'

'If you saw him again, would you recognise him? Was it this man?' He held up a picture of Lowery Powell.

'No—'

He pulled out a picture of Jason, then an old picture of a criminal-era Gavin Thomas. 'Or either of these?'

'I don't know.'

'Could you describe him?'

Vanessa, openly crying now, nodded. 'Yes,' she said.

'I've seen that face every night since. It's there, whenever I close my eyes.'

'Who was it?'

'I don't know,' Vanessa said again. 'The man … the man … he was wearing a clown mask.'

Coulrophobia. The irrational fear of clowns. Supposedly the tenth most common phobia in the UK. Slim had to admit, he wasn't fond of the things, but hearing Vanessa's words, he couldn't even begin to understand what trauma it might have caused.

'Did he see you?' Slim asked, after convincing Vanessa to let him buy her a coffee from a McDonalds drive-through before pulling into a space on a street bordering a park.

'I was coming up the service stairs at the back. I had an armful of freshly folded towels to put in the second floor airing cupboard. He … he came out of the resident's room backwards, as though to close the door quietly. I ducked into a doorway as he turned around, and he looked down the corridor, right towards me. I can only assume he couldn't see so well in the mask, because he turned and walked away.'

'Whose room did he come out of?'

Vanessa took a deep, hoarse breath. 'Carrie Thompson's.'

'You're sure?'

'Yes. They had name labels in a little plastic holder on the doors, although a couple had fallen off and needed refixing.'

'Which way did he go?'

'He went up the stairs, to the top floor. He was making a kind of growling sound, as though he were angry about something. I heard him go up there, then I heard the distinct click of a door creaking. There was one door at the top of the stairs which had a hinge that needed oiling. There was a resident in that room called Mr. Porter, but I know his label had come off, because I had picked it up myself. I heard the door close again a few seconds later, then nothing else.'

'What did you do?'

Vanessa's hands were shaking so much she was spilling the coffee. Slim took it from her and placed it into a cup holder on the dashboard.

'Vanessa?'

'The store room door was unlocked. It was full of toiletries, that kind of thing. There wasn't much space, but I sat down on the floor and pulled the door closed as far as I could. And I stayed there until he had gone. I couldn't move. I was totally, utterly paralysed.'

'How do you know he had gone?'

'Because he came back down a few minutes later. He walked past the door. But … he didn't just walk past. The door was ajar. Just a little. An inch. And he stopped, right outside. And he just stood there. And … and to this day I don't know if he knew I was there or not, but I—I—'

Vanessa started to cry again. Slim reached out a tentative hand to her and she folded into his arms.

'It wasn't your fault,' Slim said. 'You did nothing wrong.'

Vanessa began to struggle, and Slim realised she was pushing away from him. He let go as Vanessa leaned back and opened the car door.

'You don't understand,' she said. 'Nobody does. He was looking for me. I know he was!'

She must have already undone her belt, because she jumped out of the car and was off running across the park before Slim could get a grip on the situation. He tried to follow but his belt jerked and he wasted precious seconds trying to get out of the car. By the time he had made it over the pavement and into the park, Vanessa had reached the other side. He watched her run across the road into a side street and knew he would never catch her.

There were so many more questions he had to ask, yet he had now lost an opportunity. It might not be easy to get her to talk again, although he planned to try in a few days after giving her some time to calm down.

He went back to the car and sat for a long time staring out of the windscreen until the rain, which had been pattering all afternoon, began to get harder, until finally he could see nothing at all.

31

So MANY QUESTIONS. So many in fact, that he made a list. The clown mask was such a total cliché that it would have made him smile were it not that the wearer had likely left two old women dead. Yet, even with such a disguise, there were so many more possible identifying marks, if only Slim could jog Vanessa's memory. How tall had the man been? His build? Had he stood straight or walked with a stoop? His footfalls, had they been heavy or light? Had he limped? What else had he been wearing? Shoes? Gloves? And when he stood outside the store room Vanessa had cowered inside, had there been any kind of smell? An identifying aftershave, or even a "work" smell, which might have identified his occupation?

Slim was left kicking himself for letting the emotion of the situation take over. If he had kept his wits and stuck to the techniques in which he had been trained, he might have discovered something that could have identified the killer. The clown mask alone was worthless; it could have come from anywhere and been a simple ruse to direct attention towards the circus.

He drove back towards Meadow Cross. The traffic was heavy due to the rush hour and the rain, so halfway he stopped in a leisure centre car park, pulled up by a hedge, leaned his seat back and closed his eyes, going over in his mind what he knew.

The man had come out of Carrie's room and gone upstairs. He had stayed up there for a few minutes, during which time Vanessa had heard him open and close the door of a room belonging to a resident called Mr. Porter.

Some minutes of silence later, he had returned downstairs, pausing by the store room door for a while before continuing down to the ground floor.

Vanessa, understandably, had believed his focus to have been on her, but if the store room she had mentioned was the one he remembered seeing from his tour of Oak House, it was obvious what had happened.

The man had likely heard or suspected movement downstairs, and was waiting for the coast to clear. Had he known Vanessa was hiding inside the store room, the uncertainty of her reaction would almost certainly have triggered a different action on his part, depending on the callousness of the individual. An opportunistic killer would likely have panicked and fled, while one more methodical may have made Vanessa into a third victim. Vanessa might still be living through an extended trauma, but Slim had no doubt how lucky she had been.

As for the reason why the man in the clown mask had gone upstairs after coming out of Carrie's room, that was even more obvious.

It was time, Slim knew, to pay another visit to David Bellingham, this one with a little more pressure applied than before.

He had made it as far as Hagley when his phone

buzzed. He pulled over to the side of the road, then picked it up and answered.

'Slim, it's Don.'

'Don, good to hear from you.'

'I hope things are going well, Slim. I got you the address for Jason's family in Bath. Do you want me to email it, or do you have a pen handy?'

Slim opened the glovebox, then turned on the interior light. 'Got one,' he said.

'Okay …' Don read the address, then again to make sure Slim had got everything. 'I've also got a couple of phone numbers, one for a home phone and another for the father's mobile.'

Slim wrote them all down, then thanked Don and hung up. While he was stopped, he called Steve to pass the information on.

'Thanks,' Steve told him. 'I'll get in touch.'

'I'd do it carefully,' Slim said. 'You don't know what a shock it might cause. Perhaps call them first?'

'I'll be careful,' Steve said. 'I really appreciate your help.'

'I hope it works out,' Slim said. 'By the way, while we're talking, can I ask you a couple of questions?'

'Sure.'

'Did your dad have any obvious scars? On his face or anything?'

Steve gave a dry chuckle. 'He had less than either me or Mum by the time he was done with us,' he said. 'Although nothing much. There was a little scar above one eye, but that was all. And I never saw anything on his body. He'd broken an arm at some point because there was a scar on his elbow, but I think he'd done it when he was a child because it was a long incision type. They barely break the skin these days, do they?'

Slim didn't know much about medical procedures so muttered a halfhearted agreement. 'So, nothing that really stood out then?'

In his frustration, Slim realised he was dredging for scraps. If Steve had undergone the upbringing he claimed, it was likely he would never have had long conversations with his father. 'Is there anything at all you can remember him telling you about when he first arrived in the US?'

There was a pause. Then Steve said, 'Nothing much. Like I say, we didn't have a good relationship. There was one thing he said once that stayed with me. I'm not sure why. He wasn't even talking to me, but to my mother, and they were arguing about something. She was complaining about money, taxes or something. I don't remember what exactly, because I was in my room, trying to drown them out. But he said something that sounded almost boastful. He told her he had arrived with money, and he would die with it.'

32

S<small>LIM</small> <small>WAS</small> afraid of reading too much into what was a throwaway comment recalled as hearsay, but if there was any truth in Jason's words at all, that he had arrived in America with money, then it aroused his suspicion. Where had an underpaid—possibly unpaid—circus performer, likely left for dead, got the kind of money worth boasting to his spouse about?

It was yet another question to add to a growing list.

Finally making it back to Meadow Cross, Slim asked Jane to make him a sandwich and then ate it upstairs in his room. His body, surviving on caffeine and adrenaline, was dog tired, but his mind was firing with possibilities and he knew he could never sleep, even if he tried.

It was nearly nine o'clock, the last light fading from the sky, when he headed out on foot. He knew he had to be swift, decisive, and if necessary, aggressive. In the bad old days, he might have needed a drink to steel his nerves, but now he walked with the kind of cold nervousness of a man walking a tightrope, one confident in his ability yet aware that within the risks of his profession there was always that element of potential catastrophe. In a few minutes he would know whether he had made it across, or crashed to the ground below.

The road up to Oak House was lit by infrequent street lights. A curl of fairy lights wrapped around a tree beside the car park was perhaps designed to provide an element of cheer. Slim kept to the shadows as long as he could, only stepping out into the light when he had no choice.

He hadn't planned for electronically sealed doors, but as he walked up the steps to the front entrance, he realised he had made yet another misjudgment. Of course they had them. After all, two women had been murdered by an intruder able to walk inside unchallenged.

Instead, to his frustration, he stood on the step and rang the bell. For a few nervous seconds he waited, half expecting to hear sirens rise in the distance. Then, an electronic buzz sounded and a woman's voice said, 'Yes? I'm afraid visiting hours are over.'

'My name is John Hardy. I was passing and hoped to have a brief word with Mr. Bellingham, if I may. It's about my … aunt.'

'Okay, well hang on a minute,' came the awkward reply. 'I'll see if he's still up.'

As the voice cut off, Slim drummed his fingers on the door's glass panel and tapped his foot on the step. He needed to leave, to get out of here. He was pushing too hard, trying to press the investigation forward faster than was necessary. He could almost imagine his stomach filled with booze, telling him to do something irrational, like pick up a rock and fling it at the door—

'Mr. Hardy?'

'Mr. Bellingham will see you in his office.' The door's security alarm clicked, and the door slid open.

Slim went inside, his heart unnaturally thundering as

he walked up the corridor. His hands shook with the need for something to calm his nerves, and the door handle rattled as he turned it.

David Bellingham sat behind his desk, and as Slim entered, the older man held up a phone.

'I'll give you one minute to tell me why you're here,' he said. 'And then I'm calling the police.'

Slim sat down. He could have made a grab for the phone, but what would have been the point? He leaned back in the chair, waiting for his heartbeat to slow.

'I know who you are,' Bellingham said. 'One of the nurses on duty the day you visited recognised you.'

'From the television?'

Bellingham gave a mocking laugh. 'No, from the restaurant up by the church. She was there with her boyfriend one night you were there. I hadn't thought you were local, and a couple of phone calls confirmed it. I was surprised to hear that you consider yourself a private detective.'

Consider. It was an insult, but Slim let it slide.

'Two women were murdered in Oak House the night of Southern Cross Circus's final performance,' he said. 'You were running the place then, and you knew. How could you not? One of them was your own mother.'

David looked down. 'Is that what this is about? You're dredging up some thirty-year-old gossip? Haven't you got anything better to do with your time?'

'I wondered that myself. I started by looking for a missing person, and then I found him. But rather than close the door on everything, it only opened more. Sometimes I think it's a curse … but I need to know.'

'It's just a bitter rumour,' Bellingham said. 'They died of natural causes. The timing was just a cruel coincidence—'

'Your own mother was one of them,' Slim interrupted. 'Doesn't that bother you? Why would you cover up such a thing?' He leaned forward. 'I can tell you why, and it's very simple.'

'Please stop wasting my time.'

'This was your mother's business, wasn't it? And you know she would never have wanted anything to happen to it. You knew that if any truth to the rumours was discovered, your business was ruined.'

'I don't know what you're talking about—'

'You do. I have a source—'

Bellingham began to laugh, one hand tapping the tabletop. 'You found her, didn't you? And after all these years she talked. You don't really believe that rubbish, do you?'

Slim had gone over in his mind what might have happened in the aftermath of what Vanessa had seen, and decided to take a chance.

'What you paid her for her silence might have kept her quiet for a while,' he said. 'But you can't pay off the rest of someone's life.'

David Bellingham thumped the tabletop. 'The girl was hysterical. What was I supposed to do?'

Slim leaned forward. 'I can help you, David,' he said. 'I can bring your mother's killer to justice.'

David shook his head. 'I can't prove anything,' he said. 'Too much time has passed, and the end result would be the same. My business ruined. Everything my family built. Who would send their loved ones to live in corridors once stalked by a murderer?'

'But don't you want to know?'

David leaned forwards, both hands balled into fists. 'I already know. I already know. Who else could it have been? It was my brother, Robert.'

33

SLIM WENT over David Bellingham's words as he walked back to the B&B in the dark. Another jigsaw piece had seemingly moved into place, but it had an uncertain look about it, a piece of sky perhaps that was just too tight to be believed.

According to David Bellingham, his brother Robert had used the commotion at the circus as his cover, sneaking in through the rear door using a spare key. Margaret Bellingham had still been mobile at the time even while suffering from dementia. After a toilet visit, she had returned to the wrong room, laid down on Carrie Thompson's bed and fallen asleep. Later, upon this discovery, Carrie—wheelchair bound and barely cognisant —who had, as per routine, been in the television lounge downstairs, had simply been returned to Margaret's bed in exchange, with the plan to correct the mistake in the morning. Then, Robert, who had gone to Margaret's room and found a different person sleeping there, had gone looking for his mother, eventually discovering her in Carrie's room downstairs.

It was a highly callous but plausible course of action. Slim's only interaction with Robert Bellingham had left him less than impressed, and if what he had heard was true, a long-held resentment for his mother and brother could have blown over into something murderous. It was quite possible he could have used the cover of an accident at the circus to slip into Oak House and take his revenge on his mother.

Only Slim wasn't so sure. The series of events that Vanessa had described seemed to contradict what David claimed.

In Vanessa's series of events, the clown-masked killer had visited Carrie's room first.

One of them had to be wrong.

But which?

David, older, more rational, had shaped such a terrible series of events into a form he could make sense of, react to, and resolve as necessary. People died in care homes. According to David, Margaret had been suffering severe dementia, and Carrie had been wheelchair-bound and requiring 24-hour care. That both had died within minutes of each other had been made less suspicious by a separation created by the fortunate passing of midnight, something that could have been influenced by a few words of David's trusted and revered opinion.

He was protecting his mother's legacy and his business, not to mention the family name. And in his own words to Slim, 'Rotting away in prison might be what he deserves, but is it what my mother deserves? Or I? It's not just the person who commits the crime who suffers.'

Slim could only agree. Despite David's pleading that he walk away and leave things be, the best that Slim could offer was a promise to keep what he knew to himself.

It was nearly midnight when he returned to the B&B.

Jane was unhappy to have to come down and unlock the door for him, and this time he was able to make a promise in good faith, that he would try to return by eleven in future.

After making a strong coffee in his room, he slumped into a chair and stared out through the open curtains at the distant rise of the Cloverdale Hills, silhouetted against the moonlit night, his head buzzing with ideas.

Everything was a tangled mess. Nothing seemed to make any sense, even though he was uncovering new leads on a daily basis. Surely eventually he would find that elusive breakthrough?

He opened his computer to check his emails. There were no new messages except a couple of circulars, so he went through what Don had sent him. Pictures of Jason. Lowery Powell's boarding pass and landing card. He stared at the scrawled handwriting, wondering where the man might have gone after landing in Malaga, then frowned.

Hardly able to take his eyes off the screen, he reached for his bag and the collection of circus trinkets he had picked up in Stourbridge. His hands closed over the programme and he turned to the page with Lowery Powell's signature.

He wasn't an expert, but even to his eye the two signatures appeared different. Slim's heart hammered. *He* wasn't an expert, but he knew someone who was.

It was nearly one in the morning. It was pretty likely Kay Skelton, a friend who worked as a forensic linguist, would be sleeping. But just in case he wasn't, Slim made the call, pressing the old Nokia against his ear, almost willing Kay to answer.

34

HE WAS LATE DOWN in the morning, but with no other customers, Jane had set aside a couple of slices of cold toast and a bowl of cornflakes.

'And don't worry, Mr. Hardy, I saved you the dregs from yesterday's coffee pot. I'll put them in the microwave. How hot would you like them?'

'Hot enough to scald.'

Jane smiled. 'Coming right up.'

When she returned a couple of minutes later, she asked whether Slim had spoken to Vanessa yet.

'I did,' he said, unsure how much detail to give. 'It was quite a story.'

'Do you believe it?'

He shrugged. 'I'm not sure.'

'That poor girl was never the same after working there. Perhaps you could help her … you know, if you find out the truth.'

'I don't know. It was all a long time ago.'

'Well, I wish you luck. I imagine it was nice for her just to talk to someone about it.'

Slim remembered Vanessa running away across the park. He had tried to call her twice since and received no answer.

'Maybe,' he said.

After breakfast, he went back up to his room and took out the video player he had bought in the bric-a-brac shop. When he switched it on, however, he realised it was missing a wire that he needed to connect it to the TV. He could order one online, but again it would take a few days. Frustrated, he carried the player downstairs and loaded it into his car. Before heading for Stourbridge, he went across to the Spar, hoping to speak to Jessica or Derek, but instead an old woman was working alone behind the counter.

Slim was standing by the coffee machine, waiting for it to brew, when the door opened and a delivery man in a green uniform came in. He marched up to the counter, set a large package down, and said, 'Jessica Dean? Can you sign here?'

The old woman chuckled. 'She's off today. I think that's just her monthly cat food delivery, so she won't mind if I sign.'

The delivery man smiled. 'Just make it a bit of a scribble,' he said.

'Sure.'

After the man had left, the old woman put the package down behind the counter, then glanced at Slim. 'Don't tell anyone, will you?'

Slim smiled. 'Not a word.'

He went out, only realising what he had heard as he got back to his car.

Jessica Dean. She had to be Kevin Dean's ex-wife. He had wanted to speak to Derek's father before, but that he had been the same man who had driven up to the

Cloverdale Hills so that Gavin Thomas could take his revenge on Jason Felton, made him a key person.

Slim walked up the road to Katie Julius's house, and found her in her front garden, watering the flowers.

'Good morning,' she said cheerfully, and Slim gave a wry smile. Not everyone was mired in the dark secrets of the past.

'I wanted to ask a favour,' Slim said.

Katie put down her watering can and stood up. 'If I can help, Slim. What's up?'

'Your friend Jessica … I'd like to get in touch with her ex-husband. Kevin, isn't it?'

'Is this part of your investigation?'

'Yes, maybe. I'd just like to ask him a question or two.'

Katie pulled off a pair of gardening gloves and set them down beside the watering can.

'All right. So I guess you're after his number? I might have it written down somewhere. Hang on a mo.'

She went inside. Slim waited, the sun warming his face. Katie had a pretty garden, the flowerbeds well-tended. After a moment he sighed. He wasn't so far off retirement age. Maybe one day—

'Here you go,' Katie said, returning with a slip of paper. 'If you don't mind, don't tell him who gave it to you. I know him and Jessica are still pretty close. She'd have a— how do you Brits say?—a strop if she knew I was handing out his number to a detective.'

'I'm not a real one,' Slim said. 'So it's okay.'

'You're close enough.'

'Thanks.'

'Good luck.'

Slim returned to the B&B and drove into Stourbridge. He found a café near the town centre where he made the call, but got only a voicemail. He left Dean a message and was about to call Kay to follow up on last night, when his phone buzzed, Steve's name and number flashing up on the display.

'Steve? This is Slim.'

'Hey, Slim. I just wanted to let you know I got in touch with my grandparents. I went down to see them last night. They told me something about Dad that I thought I ought to pass it on. It might be nothing, but it might help.'

'Sure. I appreciate you thinking of me.'

'Well, it turns out you were wrong about Dad, and I was right.'

Slim's heart began to thunder. 'What do you mean?'

'Like I say, it's probably not gonna help you much, but it turns out that when he told me he was brought up in foster care, it was more or less true. The Feltons weren't Dad's real parents. He was an orphan. He'd been through several foster homes, but with the Feltons, he got lucky. They adopted him.'

35

Steve had no further information, and told Slim that Jason's adoptive parents hadn't been willing to give details about Jason's background prior to the adoption. After Steve hung up, Slim called Don.

'That explains it,' Don said. 'I couldn't find anything on his early life, but if he was adopted, the records would be sealed. I'll see if I can find anything, now that I have a lead. Give me a couple of days.'

'Thanks, Don,' Slim said, and hung up.

Slim tried Vanessa again, but again got no answer. Instead, he headed for an electrical store in search for a video player connector wire. The customer service worker told him they had none in stock, but he would make a phone call and try to get one in for the following morning.

Slim decided to wait around in Stourbridge in case Kevin Dean called after work. It had started to rain and there was a limit to the amount of coffee even he could drink, so he headed back to Stourbridge Public Library, where he borrowed a computer to do a little of his own research.

Even with what he had unearthed, there was still little go on. He knew many people might have been pleased just to have found Jason, but for Slim that was just the start of the mystery.

Sometimes it was easier to line up what he could confirm.

According to Gavin, Jason had got his girlfriend at the time pregnant. Elaine Baxter had since died in a way Slim was yet to discover.

Gavin had gone to Southern Cross Circus to find Jason. Along with several acquaintances, they had first roughed Jason up, then taken Jason up to the Cloverdale Hills, where Gavin had finished the job, leaving Jason for dead before returning to the circus on foot.

First, Slim needed to confirm what Gavin had told him. Kevin Dean might be able to help with that, as might the contents of the VHS tape Derek had lent him, once he was able to play it.

Had that happened before or after Maria's fall, however? Had it happened before, it would rule Jason out as responsible for both that and the murders of Margaret and Carrie, which Vanessa claimed had happened later at night.

His prime suspect for those was currently Robert Bellingham, but even that made little sense. Surely he couldn't have made a mistake and killed the wrong person? Unless … Slim tapped a finger on the tabletop and gave a slow nod. Unless that had been a way to throw people off the scent. Had there ever been an inquest into the two deaths, putting the blame on some anonymous circus worker would have been easy, leaving Robert in the clear.

But what if … Slim's train of thought was broken by his phone buzzing. He snatched it up from the tabletop, giving a nervous glance over his shoulder, but the librarian was nowhere nearby.

'Yes?'

'Slim, it's me. Kay.'

'Kay?'

'I have to say, I'm thankful that for once you've given me something to deal with that's within my area of expertise. I had a look at those two samples you sent me.'

'Do they match?'

'Even allowing for the fact that when people are filling out those landing cards they're not really giving it any great concentration … they don't match at all. The person who filled out that landing card was not the same person who signed that circus programme.'

36

'EVEN IF YOU can get me a complete list of names, it could take weeks to find out something like that,' Don said. 'I'll do what I can, but don't get your hopes up.'

'You know I appreciate it, Don.'

Don sighed. 'Get me a list, Slim. But no promises.'

Passports were pretty complex these days, but thirty years ago, they had been a little easier to fake or alter. Even so, to have faked Lowery Powell's travel to Malaga added a whole new angle to the investigation. It implied forethought and planning, and raised another question: if Powell hadn't gone to Malaga, then where was he?

Slim tried Kevin again, but got no answer, so reluctantly headed back to Meadow Cross. Due to an accident, he found himself caught in a traffic jam on Hagley Road, so with no other leads to act on, he called Maria.

'Slim, hi.' She sounded tired, disappointed to hear from him.

'Hi, Maria. I'm sorry to bother you. I know you're

probably sick of hearing from me, but I have a couple of questions about Jason.'

There was a long pause. Then Maria said, 'Okay, Slim. If you're not going to let this go, then what do you want to know?'

'I wondered if you knew Jason was adopted.'

Maria chuckled. 'Huh. Was he? No, I had no idea. How do you dig such things up, Slim?'

'I must be lucky. So he never mentioned it?'

'Ours wasn't the deepest relationship when it came to conversation,' Maria said. 'It was more … you know, physical.'

'Did you know Jason had other lovers?'

Maria chuckled again. 'Are you trying to make me feel even worse than I do already?'

'No, it's just—'

'Of course I knew,' Maria said, voice dripping with bitterness. 'And I *hated* it. He was always full of excuses about where he'd been, who he'd been with. I knew he was lying, but what could I do? I loved him, Slim.'

'Did you ever confront him about it?'

'I was barely out of school. He told me he loved me, that he wanted to be with me. He was full of it, but I was smitten. I believed anything he said. And I think … I think he meant some of it. I think he did love me. He was just young, good-looking, and girls were throwing themselves at him. I don't think he could resist the attention.'

'Did you know any of them by name?'

'No.'

'Did you ever hear the name Elaine Baxter?'

Maria coughed. 'Yeah, but he … wouldn't have. She was Gavin's girlfriend.'

'Gavin Thomas?'

'Yeah.'

Slim said nothing. Best to let Maria talk. After a moment of silence, she continued, 'Elaine was his girlfriend. She was all right. She was working on one of the stalls. I don't know, the candy floss or the shooting gallery, something like that. Jason would never have touched her.'

'Why not?'

'For a start because Gavin would have killed him. And I don't mean to be rude, but she wasn't all that. She was nice enough to be around, but she wasn't much of a looker, if you know what I mean. Plus, for the whole time I was working at Southern Cross Circus, Jason and Gavin were the best of mates.'

37

SLIM'S HEAD was still ringing with Maria's words when he finally made it back to Meadow Cross. After two hours stuck in a car on Hagley Road, he was keen to stretch out his legs, so he left the car at the B&B and walked down Meadow Cross Lane until he came to the farm track that led into the field behind Oak House and the site of Southern Cross Circus. Safely off the property of either Bellingham brother, he climbed up into the hedge from where he had a decent vantage point, pulled out his pocket camera and took a couple of dozen photographs of the site and the nearby houses. Nothing stood out as suspicious or irregular, but perhaps something might trigger an idea later when he had loaded them up onto his laptop.

He headed back up the road, and went into the Spar to buy a sandwich for dinner. Derek was working behind the counter, and smiled as Slim came in.

'I took your advice,' he said.

'What?'

'I got Helen a book. She liked it.'

Slim smiled. 'I'm glad. What about the coffee?'

'She said she's officially non-caffeine.'

'Did she now?'

'She's also a vegan.'

'She must be a hassle to take out.'

Derek shrugged. 'If I get that far.'

'Keep working on it.'

Slim picked up a few items for dinner then returned to the counter.

'Could I ask a favour?'

'Uh … what?'

'I'd like to have a word with your dad.'

'Dad? Why, what's he got to do with anything?'

'Nothing much. I just have a couple of questions. I called him, but he's not returning my calls.'

'Is he in trouble?'

Slim chuckled. 'Not at all.'

'All right, I'll ask him.'

'Thanks. If you could just get him to call me back, that would be great. I only need five minutes of his time.'

Slim paid for his shopping and went back to the B&B. Upstairs in his room, he loaded the photos he had taken of the circus site onto his laptop, then browsed through them for a few minutes, looking for something that stood out.

There was nothing he could see that really helped him at all. Oak House looked like it always had, stately and majestic. The patch of waste ground was just that, a weed-strewn area of nothing. On the other side, Robert's cottage was partially hidden by trees. The quaint roof of the original building was somewhat ruined by the flat roof of the modern extension beside it. Slim peered closer, noting a set of stairs descending at the side of the extension, probably leading to a cellar. While he couldn't see clearly from the picture, it didn't look like there was any kind of rail or support for a man who walked with a stick. Katie had said Robert claimed to be terminally ill; it might be worth mining some medical records for a little more information.

Looking again at the photographs of the waste ground, Slim wondered why Robert hadn't sold it off or done something else with it. It wasn't so junk strewn or overgrown as to create an eyesore for the residents of Oak House; in fact, besides from the upper floor windows it would be barely visible behind the trees of the house gardens.

Katie had also suggested that Robert had allowed Southern Cross Circus to use the land in order to get back at his brother. It now seemed that Lowery Powell, like Jason, had vanished in mysterious circumstances. Did Robert know something? Was he somehow involved?

Slim had wanted to ask Maria more about the chaotic days following the circus's abrupt dissolution, but Maria had known little.

'I was in hospital for nearly a month,' she had said. 'And after that I was in rehabilitation, basically learning to walk again. I wanted nothing to do with that circus nor anyone involved with it.'

'Did no one visit you?'

'No one. I was moved to a spinal unit down in London. By the time I was even aware the circus had shut down, everyone had left and the site had been cleared. It was as though it had never existed.'

'But who told you?'

Maria went quiet, and Slim wondered if she'd hung up.

'I received a letter,' she said at last.

'Who from?'

Maria sniffed, and Slim squeezed his eyes shut, hating himself for what he was doing to her.

'From Lowery.'

'Do you still have it?'

'In a box somewhere. Maybe. Let me guess, you want a copy.'

'I—'

'I'll have a look, Slim.' She sniffed again. 'Please Slim, let this go. You don't need to keep digging. Just … let it go.'

They had ended the call shortly after. Slim had kept himself busy since, avoiding dwelling on the harder parts of their conversation, instead concentrating on those parts that helped his investigation.

He was getting a headache, but still couldn't stop digging. Needing to pull himself back from the edge a little, however, he went on to a long unused social media page and searched for an Elaine Baxter. His search returned about twenty results in the UK, so Slim wrote out a brief message and sent it to all of the profiles not set to private.

Hello, my name is John Hardy. I'm a detective investigating an historical cold case. If you were associated with a man named Gavin Thomas in the Hagley/Stourbridge area in the late 80s/early 90s, please get in touch.

A supposed man of the cloth he might be, but despite the conviction in his words, Slim was now convinced Gavin Thomas was lying.

38

IN THE MORNING, the electrical store in Stourbridge called to say they had managed to get the wire Slim needed, so he drove into town to collect it. He was keen to get back to the B&B to watch the VHS tape, but just as he was leaving, his phone buzzed. He pulled the car over to the roadside and checked the number. It wasn't one stored in his phone book so he called back.

'Hello?' came a man's voice Slim didn't recognise.

'This is Slim Hardy.'

'Ah, right. The boy told me your name. He … ah … said you wanted a word. This is Kevin Dean.'

'Right. Do you have a minute now?'

'Ah … I'm at work. Can I call you at lunchtime?'

'Sure.'

'All right.'

Kevin hung up. Slim checked his watch. At a little after eleven, there was still time to get back to the B&B and watch the VHS tape before Kevin called back. Aware Kevin was likely to feature in it, he had a chance to compile a few questions.

The traffic accident that had delayed him yesterday had thankfully been cleared up, and he found himself back in Meadow Cross half an hour later.

There was a tiny TV in his room, but it had no port for the wire he had painstakingly acquired. Instead, he went downstairs, wondering if he could use the larger television in the breakfast room.

The B&B felt empty and deserted. Often, when he was back during the day, he would find Jane in the kitchen or hoovering one of the downstairs rooms, but today it seemed she had gone out. Slim went into the empty breakfast room where the television stood on a chest of drawers in the corner.

He had to place a chair in front for the video player, but the television had the required wire port and after a few frustrated minutes of flicking through channels and pressing buttons, he managed to get the video to play. Slim pulled up a chair and sat down to watch.

The first scene was of the darkening skies in the distance over the Cloverdale Hills. The camera jerked back and forth soundlessly. Slim turned up the volume, but it appeared that either the tape's age or operating incompetence had left the video without sound. The camera turned, the image blurring, then focused on the smiling face of a young man Slim could immediately tell was Derek's father. He was walking along Meadow Cross Lane. He lifted a hand and gave a shy wave, then reached out for the camera. The screen went blank.

Moments later, another scene appeared. This one was from inside the Big Top, and swung over a sizable crowd as they shuffled into their seats. Kevin appeared to be holding the camera as now Jessica's face appeared close by, wearing a grin. She waved, then flapped a hand towards the circus ring as the lights went down. With everything on screen happening in silence, accompanied by only the occasional click and hum of the old video player, the scene was almost dreamlike. Slim found himself smiling at the sight of a line of acrobats marching through a break in the curtains on the far side of the ring, fanning out to the sides as they waved at the crowd. Feeling as though he was watching memories from an alternative version of his own childhood, it was something of a shock when the camera suddenly twisted to show Kevin looking away, talking to a tall man who was leaning over him. The camera twisted, the screen going blank.

Slim stopped the tape and rewound it, replaying the section and pausing it several times until he was certain of the identity of the man standing over Kevin. It wasn't easy to tell that this overbearing, angry man would turn into a man of God, but Gavin Thomas had the same jawline, the same shape of nose.

Slim allowed the film to play forward for a while, watching a couple of short scenes of various tumbling and acrobatic performances. Even without any spoken commentary, the way the camera jerked about gave the impression of being halfhearted. For one moment it turned to show the empty seat where Kevin had been sitting, as though to make sure that on viewing a playback he would remember how he had bailed on the date.

Then the scene changed. The view moved along the back of the crowd, the right side blurry with shadow, the inner side too bright from the circus lights. It created a creepy, hallucinogenic effect that made Slim frown as he wondered what Jessica was doing. She slipped out of the circus tent and for a few seconds the view was nothing but darkness punctuated by occasional bright lights Slim guessed came from stalls and stands outside the big top, but without proper lighting it was impossible to be sure. Slim wondered if Jessica was going home, then the light plumed again as she went back through a curtain.

At the sight of performers standing around or sitting on chairs in various states of dress, Slim understood. Jessica had sneaked backstage, trying to capture a little of the circus's inner workings. Someone waved at her, while another flapped a hand to shoo her away. As she turned, a young girl hurried across the back of the view and out through a fold in the tent. At first Slim thought it was Maria, but her hair was fair while Maria's had been dark brown in the other video. Then the camera twisted as a bright green hand closed over the lens, pushing it downwards. Jessica backed up and the view cleared. A red-nosed, purple-cheeked clown gesticulated wildly, his painted face comically angry. A man sitting behind him on a chair seemed amused as he watched the exchange while strapping a long wooden stilt to one leg. Then the screen went blank.

The next scene to appear was one of chaos. Jessica was back in her seat, but standing up, trying to see over the crowd in front of her. Someone was lying on the ground in the middle of the ring, surrounded by other performers. A tall man in a top hat appeared to wave at someone in the crowd before turning and marching out through the curtains at the rear. The view zoomed in a little, and through the moving legs of the gathered performers, Slim saw a patch of dark brown hair, a head writhing back and forth in agony. Then the camera twisted, revealing Kevin, who was shaking his head and waving his hands from side to side, as he spoke silently. Slim had no lip-reading skills, but his words were obvious:

'Turn it off. Turn it off.'

The scene went blank, and after a few seconds the screen turned white again. Slim let the tape run for a couple more minutes until it reached the end, but there was nothing more.

He switched the television off and sat back, staring at the blank screen, the scenes still playing over in his mind. So much to digest. The film not only put a timeline on Gavin and Kevin's jaunt up to the Cloverdale Hills, but also caught the aftermath of Maria's accident. Jessica had missed the exact moment of the fall but maybe there was something hidden in the scene that might give Slim a clue as to what had happened.

He was just about to watch the tape again when the front door opened sharply and then slammed shut. Footsteps in the hall were followed by a shout of 'Mr. Hardy? Mr. Hardy? Are you there?'

'I'm here,' he called, standing up.

Jane Cornick appeared in the doorway, her face flushed with anger.

'There you are, thank goodness. What did you say to her? What did you say to our Vanessa? I just got back from the hospital. This morning she tried to kill herself.'

39

JANE DIDN'T WANT to hear excuses or explanations and demanded that he leave immediately. While he was upstairs packing, however, she abruptly burst into his room, her eyes filled with tears, and asked him to stop. She sat down on the bed, and he found himself sitting with an arm around her while she sobbed against his chest.

'She cut her wrists in the toilet cubicle at her work,' she said. 'One of the other staff found her and called the ambulance. She's alive but unconscious. I don't know if … if she'll make it.'

He stayed silent, comforting her while she told versions of the same events as though trying to make sense of it. She talked about how Vanessa had changed after what she claimed to have seen in Oak House, self-destructive tendencies resulting in poor choices of friends and partners, her life a long and extended downward spiral for which this felt like the absolute bottom.

It would have been easy for Slim to roll out the analysis, that she was probably a long-term sufferer of PTSD and that cutting her wrists where someone would likely find her was a cry for help, but he didn't want to be a textbook. Jane needed a presence, something to absorb her suffering, so he stared out of the bedroom window at the Cloverdale Hills, tears in his own eyes until she had cried herself out. Finally, she pulled a tissue from her pocket, wiped her eyes, and looked up.

'I didn't mean it,' she said. 'You can stay. This … this … could have happened anyway.'

'I'm sorry,' Slim said.

Jane stood up. 'I need to get on,' she said. 'This place won't run itself, will it? I have more guests due this evening.' She shook her head. 'Oh, the timing of it….'

'If there's anything I can help with….'

Jane gave him a resilient smile. 'Do you know how to change a bed?'

'I was in the Armed Forces for a while,' he said. 'It was one of the first things they taught us.'

Jane stood up. 'Okay, well, if you can help with that, I can sort out the towels….'

'Would you please keep me up to date with Vanessa's condition?' Slim asked. 'And when'—he chose his words carefully—'she wakes up, I'd love the opportunity to visit her. I'd like to tell her too that I'm sorry.'

Jane smiled and nodded, then backed out of the room without meeting his eyes, as though everything had been a misunderstanding.

Slim, aching with guilt, was happy to help out in any way he could to keep his mind off an unconscious Vanessa lying in a hospital bed, although eventually Jane told him she needed nothing more. He was happy to go out and get some fresh air.

Across the street, the doors of a pub taunted him, so he made a point of walking the other way, up the road to the church, where he sat on a bench outside and stared at his hands, unable to think of anything other than Vanessa. His phone had rung twice, but he couldn't bring himself to pick it up. More than ever before he wished he had taken Maria's advice and walked away. Now it was too late. A young woman was in hospital, and might die because of his persistence.

He was still sitting there when a car pulled up, parking lazily near the hedge a short distance away. A disabled sticker was displayed in the front window, and a moment later the door opened and Robert Bellingham got out. He adjusted his sweater, then leaned in and quite easily retrieved a walking stick from inside. He slammed the car door and had taken a few steps with the stick under his arm before he noticed Slim sitting on the bench. Their eyes met. Robert frowned, then lowered the stick and made a point of limping up the road past Slim, until he reached the churchyard gate. There, he paused, turned back, and snapped, 'What are you looking at?'

Slim just sighed. He was tempted to say nothing, but some last breath of defiance rose up inside him as he said, 'My own mother was as worthless as they came. Still, even if given the chance, I don't think I could have killed her. It must have taken some level of hatred to have held that pillow over your mother's face, Robert. Or was it mercy? Were you trying to put her out of her misery?'

Robert's face flushed with anger. He lifted the stick and Slim wondered if he might throw it down then come rushing over, fists clenched. Instead, after a long moment of stalemate, he tapped it against the wall of the gate and shook his head.

'I don't know who you are, but I've seen you wandering around. You and your lies and accusations are not wanted here.'

Slim gave a weak smile. His body wanted to sleep, but

his tongue was on a roll.

'It was easy, wasn't it? In the chaos when that girl fell from her trapeze, you sneaked in there, didn't you? It was easy because you had a key. But killing your own mother wasn't enough, was it? In order to divert suspicion, you killed another woman, too, didn't you? An innocent, forgotten woman who had done nothing wrong?'

Robert stared at him. 'Are you drunk?'

'I sometimes wish I was.'

'I don't have time for this rubbish. Good day to you.'

He pushed in through the churchyard gate, muttering to himself, not looking back. Slim mustered enough motivation to push himself up to his feet and head on up the road. He wasn't ready to go back to the B&B yet, but when he did he wondered if there might be something interesting to hear on the discreet microphone Alan Coaker had provided, which he had hidden by Margaret Bellingham's grave. Having riled Robert, there would be no better time for a graveside confession.

That was if he could bring himself to do anything at all. With his back bent like a man twice his age, he struggled up the footpath to the Cloverdale Hills, panting as he reached the stone circle at the top. There, he didn't even bother to find a bench, just sat, and then lay down on the grass, the wind ruffling the collar of his jacket as he stared up at the sky, wondering why he couldn't just walk away. He was close, he knew it. He was close to figuring out the answers. But at what cost?

His phone buzzed in his pocket. He ignored it, but a minute later it buzzed again. When it buzzed a third time, he could no longer resist. He pulled the phone from his pocket and pressed it to his ear.

'Slim? It's Don. I've found something. I'm sending it over now. You're going to want to see this.'

40

BACK IN HIS room at the B&B, Slim found two new emails from Don. One contained a scanned document related to Jason Felton. The text was too small to read clearly, but from what Slim could decipher, Jason had been the youngest child of three who had been taken into care in 1975 following the death of their parents in a car accident. With no relatives to care for them, they had been placed into a foster home outside Birmingham.

While in foster care, however, a tragic accident had befallen his older sister, and afterwards, Jason's behavior had spiraled out of control. The report was a list of misdemeanours: reported issues at school, violence towards other foster children and adult staff, vandalism, petty crime. It painted a fledgling picture of the adult Steve had described, although after being moved to a foster family in Bath, where he had later been adopted, it appeared the troubles had stopped. The last report, from when Jason was fifteen, claimed he was "adapting well to his new environment" and "continuing to make positive progress".

A keen interest in sport, particularly gymnastics, was "absorbing much of his destructive energy.'

Slim was about to open the other email when a new one from Maria appeared in his inbox. He opened it and read, "I found the letter. Please find a scan attached. Maria."

The coolness of Maria's tone was obvious, and Slim swallowed another pang of regret as he opened the attachment and brought the scanned letter up on the screen.

October 20th, 1992
Dear Maria,
I hope your recovery is going well. I can only tell you how sorry I am for what hapened to you. I have nothing but regret and can only assume there was some kind of foul play involved. As you know, all our ropes and harnesses are checked regularly for safety. What hapened to you was a terrible accident. Again, I'm very sorry. I hope that otherwise your time at Southern Cross Circus was an enjoyable one. I'm afraid that after your accident, I was forced to close the circus, and sell off its remaining assets to pay company costs. The last days were a hard time for us all, believe me. I'm sorry I can't tell you more, but there's nothing else to say except I wish you all the best for the future.
Yours faithfully
Lowery Powell

Slim read the letter twice, then emailed a copy to Kay, asking for him to check it against the other samples. Noting the date, Slim emailed Maria, asking if she still had the envelope in order to check the postmark, but she quickly replied to say she no longer had it.

His stomach grumbled, reminding him that he hadn't eaten for some hours. He went outside and drove out of town until he found a supermarket where he bought a couple of packets of sandwiches which he ate in the car. Rain streamed down the window, obscuring his view of the car park and creating a cocoon of safety inside which he felt a modicum of calm. For once his mind was blank, and after finishing his sandwiches, he put the seat back and lay down, hands behind his head. He closed his eyes, and opened them to find the rain had stopped and he was now parked in darkness.

He shook his head, clearing out the sleepiness, then switched on the engine. The car dash told him it was a little after ten p.m., so he headed back to Meadow Cross. It was unlikely he would be able to sleep until late now, but for once he felt sharp and awake. He headed upstairs, determined to push the emotion aside and rediscover the cold detective's façade that he needed to finish the investigation.

He had just sat down at the desk in his room when his phone buzzed.

'Kay?'

'Sorry to call so late, Slim, but I imagine you'd be happy to return the favour. I checked that handwriting.'

'And?'

'A couple of things. First, it matches that on the landing card. I can say almost with certainty that the person who wrote that letter is the same person who filled out that landing card before getting off a plane in Malaga.'

Slim's heart sank. So it seemed he was wrong about Lowery Powell. He had gone to Spain after all.

'One more thing.'

'Yes?'

'I did an analysis of the text, and I noticed a few things.

Now, this is the speculative part of what I do, and I'd like to point out that this would be highly unlikely to hold up in court.'

'Sure.'

'Well, it's very formally written in places. Almost too much, as though it were written by a lawyer. Yet, there are basic errors a lawyer would never make. "Happened" is spelt both times with a missing P. This might seem insignificant, but all the other major words are spelled correctly, suggesting they might have been checked or copied. For "happened" to have been spelled wrong suggests a misguided confidence in the writer's ability. Then there are casual phrases such as "I'm very sorry", which jar with the more formal sections. It's subtle, but do you think a lawyer would write that? Wouldn't they use phrases like "you have my apologies"?'

'I don't know.'

'In my professional opinion, I would say that letter has not been written by the name signed at the bottom. It has been written by someone pretending to be that person, using a mixture of copied material. In short, it's fake.'

Slim took a deep breath. 'But it matches the handwriting on the landing card.'

'One hundred percent.'

41

IT WAS like a knot with no protruding ends, no place to start. Slim found himself pacing around in circles until he heard someone banging on the ceiling below. Instead, he lay on his bed and stared up at the ceiling. There was an answer somewhere, if only he could find the thread and pluck it out of the air.

Lowery Powell had disappeared. The person who had flown to Malaga under Lowery's passport had also sent the letter to Maria, but neither was Powell. After the night of September 26th, there was no evidence that Lowery Powell even existed.

Was he dead?

Or had he pulled an elaborate vanishing act?

It was too late to make any phone calls, so Slim pulled out his folders of gathered evidence and began going over it all again. After a while his eyes began to ache from all the text, so he turned instead to the photographs he had gathered, both of the current site and those historical ones Derek had given him. Surely there had to be a clue somewhere.

He rubbed his eyes. Perhaps he needed to go back to the television company's archive, watch the video segment again. He would make another call in the morning. In the meantime, he could watch the VHS tape one more time.

He looked around for the video player, realising to his frustration that he had left it downstairs. He hurried down, but was surprised to hear the sound of someone crying in the breakfast room. He cracked the door and peered through.

Jane Cornick was sitting on a chair in front of the television, wiping her eyes with a tissue as the video played back. Slim watched for a few seconds, then pushed open the door. Jane jumped up with a start, her hand going to her mouth.

'Oh, Mr. Hardy, I do apologise,' she said. 'I didn't mean to pry. I just couldn't help but wonder what you were watching, and once I started, I'm afraid I got a little lost in nostalgia.'

'It's okay,' Slim said. Unwilling to reveal his source even though Jane could likely have deduced it from the footage, he added, 'I was lucky to come across it. Were you there that night?'

'Oh no, not at all, but I recognised a few of those faces and it took me back. And then when I saw Vanessa, it just broke me. You wouldn't know it to see her now, but she was such a pretty girl. She had her whole life ahead of her.'

'Wait. Vanessa? Where?'

Jane flapped a hand at the TV. 'She was just there. Walking past in the background. I don't know why—'

Slim squatted by the video player. He rewound the tape and started the film again.

'Please show me,' he said.

'Oh, well, it was in a minute....'

The scenes scrolled past. When they reached the

section where Jessica sneaked backstage, Jane leaned forward.

'Just about … there. There she is.'

Slim stared at the young girl walking across the back of the screen, then as she disappeared out of shot, he switched the tape off. He had barely noticed her before, and hadn't recognised the girl as a much younger Vanessa. Now though, he could only wonder what she had been doing backstage at the Southern Cross Circus on a night she was supposed to have been working next door in Oak House.

And a few more jigsaw pieces fitted into place.

'Mr. Hardy? Are you all right?'

Slim nodded. 'I think so,' he said, thinking about Vanessa, lying in the hospital bed, aware that she wasn't very well at all.

42

SOMEHOW HE MUST HAVE FALLEN asleep, but he woke with a caffeine hangover to find the sun streaming in through his open curtains. He got up, looked at the clock to find he was long past breakfast time, and quickly roused himself.

A few minutes later, he headed downstairs. Jane was nowhere to be found, and the coffee machine in the breakfast room needed refilling. He had used up his own supply kept in his room, so in search of something to wake him up, he headed across the street to the Spar, where he found Jessica behind the counter, reading a magazine. She looked up as he came in, a small smile creasing her mouth.

'Our local dating expert.'

'Excuse me?'

'I don't know what you said to Derek, but he's raving about you. He and Helen are now an item, and apparently it's thanks to you.'

Slim shrugged. 'It's nice to be helping someone out for a change. I just suggested he buy her a book rather than a bottle of vodka.'

'A good choice. Perhaps you could work your magic on

the rest of the teenagers round here. I wouldn't need that camera anymore.' She leaned forward. 'So, what are you looking for, Mike? Or is it John? Or Slim?'

Slim gave her a sheepish smile, aware it was their first encounter since his slip up in the church, which now felt like a lifetime ago.

'Slim works best.'

'And have you solved the great circus mystery yet?'

Her tone was not so much mocking as humourous, as though he were some kid playing a game.

'Not yet,' he said. 'I don't suppose there's anything you can help me with?'

'I doubt it.'

'You know Gavin Thomas? Or should I say, Reverend Thomas?'

Jessica's smile dropped. 'From the church, yes.'

'I just wondered what you were doing there that day. The day of the service where I slipped up and revealed I was using an assumed name?'

Jessica gave an awkward shrug. 'I go just to offer my support. You know, to the Reverend, and the attendees.'

'And you take Derek?'

'Do you have something against religion?'

Slim shook his head. 'Not at all. I just wondered why you might be taking your teenage son to an emotional support group.'

Jessica scowled. 'I used to drink, too. After Kevin left. Not much, just enough that Derek noticed. He makes me go, not the other way round.'

'You have a good son.'

Jessica sniffed. 'Thank you. Now, did you want something?'

'Coffee, please. And do you remember Elaine Baxter? Gavin's ex-girlfriend, who died?'

Jessica stumbled as she reached the coffee machine. 'What? Elaine didn't die. She moved down to London years ago.'

'That's not what Gavin said.' Slim had received a couple of replies from women called Elaine Baxter, but none claimed to know what he was talking about.

'I still get a Christmas card from her every year,' Jessica said. 'I've probably still got the one from last Christmas if you need proof.'

Slim shook his head. 'It's all right,' he said. 'But do you think it's normal for a man of the church to lie?'

Jessica made the coffee and set it down on the counter. 'Can I give you some advice, Slim? Don't go messing with Gavin Thomas. He's a wolf in sheep's clothing. That's one pound fifty, please.'

The smoothness with which Gavin had lied to him made Slim more determined than ever to confront the supposed minister.

He headed up to the church, but found it locked. Instead, he went around to the back and retrieved the recording device Alan Coaker had sent. To his frustration, however, the rain together with an unsuspecting foot had left it partially buried in mud. He had tried to listen to the recording yesterday, but found nothing other than a few indistinct bumping sounds. With a scowl, he cleaned it off and put it in his pocket.

On the walk back to the B&B, he called Kevin—who had never called back—and left another message, then grabbed his laptop and the notes he had compiled so far before getting into his car and heading over to Hagley. It was now almost lunchtime so there was a good chance he would find Gavin Thomas at work.

When he arrived at the pub, however, it was closed, with no lights in the windows, and when he tried the front door, he found it bolted. It was evidently a surprise, as while he was waiting outside another customer came ambling up the street and went to walk inside, only to find the door locked. He muttered a curse under his breath, shrugged at Slim, then headed across the street to an off-license.

Slim waited in the car for a while, but after a couple of people had angrily shouted through the window that he was illegally parked, he decided to leave.

Only as he was driving away did he wonder whether Jessica might have tipped Gavin off. He decided to call Kevin again, but this time, he pulled up by the side of the road and went into a nearby phone box. This time Kevin answered.

'Hello?'

'Kevin? This is Slim Hardy. Is this a good time to talk?'

'Ah … not really.'

'I just have a few questions. It'll only take a minute of your time.'

'Look, I've been thinking about this and I'm not sure there's anything I can really tell you. I think it might be best if you … ah … find someone else.'

The tremble in Kevin's voice was obvious. Someone had got to him first, warning him not to speak.

'Whatever you can tell me, it stays between us,' Slim said. 'Has Gavin Thomas been in touch with you?'

'Gav? No … look, I've got to get back to work.'

Kevin didn't wait for a response. The line went dead.

Slim resisted the urge to slam the receiver against the window, instead replacing it in the cradle and returning to his car. Perhaps if he showed up at Kevin's work or home, he could get him to speak?

But, Slim knew, it no longer mattered what Kevin said. His reaction—and the possibility that someone might have pressured him into silence—told Slim as much as a confession might have.

He drove to Stourbridge. There he headed for the local council offices, a folded piece of paper in his pocket, his list of things he needed to check. There were one or two minor factual events he needed to confirm that kept getting lost in the mire of speculation, gossip, and rumour that surrounded much of the case.

After collecting the document he wanted, he headed back to the car. He had just made it when his phone buzzed. Slim lifted an eyebrow at the sight of the B&B's number.

'Yes?'

'Mr. Hardy, this is Jane. It's about Vanessa.'

For an instant Slim's heart lurched, almost making him drop the phone. Then Jane said, 'She's awake. And she asked to see you.'

43

SLIM DROVE straight over to the Birmingham hospital where Vanessa was recovering. To his frustration, he had just missed morning visiting hours and had to wait around in a café downstairs until the afternoon session began at three o'clock. Even then there was some delay as he tried to explain his reason for visiting, resulting in a call up to Vanessa's ward to get confirmation from Vanessa herself.

At last, though, Slim found himself sitting beside Vanessa's bed, a curtain pulled around them. Despite being pale and obviously weak, to Slim she actually looked better than she had the first time they had met. The nervous tension had gone, replaced by a sense of purpose. Before she had been haggard, aged beyond her years, but now the attractive woman she still was had emerged belatedly from its cocoon.

'How are you?' Slim said.

Vanessa smiled. 'I've been better.'

'I'm sorry for what happened.'

'Don't be. I think it was long overdue. Believe it or not … I actually feel a little better.'

'What happened wasn't your fault.'

'Don't say that. It was. I can't explain it, but I wrote it down for you … before. In the drawer there's a key to my flat. I taped the letter to the fridge. It felt good to write it down, even though it hurt. I'm so sorry, Slim. I won't say I never meant no harm, because I did. But … it wasn't really me. I wasn't thinking straight.'

Vanessa's eyes closed, and for one horrifying moment Slim thought she was going to die. Then she opened her eyes again and offered a weak smile.

'I'm so tired, Slim. I hope you can understand.'

A heart rate monitor began to beep and a moment later a doctor pulled back the curtain and stepped inside.

'She needs to rest,' the doctor said, and Slim took that as his cue to leave. He stood up.

'In the drawer,' Vanessa reminded him.

He had wondered how he might find where she lived, but the key conveniently had a keyring attached to it with her address written inside a plastic cover in softened biro. Back in the car, it took Slim a few minutes with a map of Birmingham before he located it a short walk from Tony's. Twenty minutes later he was standing on a fourth floor landing, outside Vanessa's front door.

He turned the key in the lock, but his hand wavered as he leaned forwards to pull the door open. The look in Vanessa's eyes still haunted him, but for reasons it had taken him time to understand. In her face he saw a version of himself reflected back: a wreck of a human being battered on treacherous rocks, clinging desperately to survival. He liked coming home to the B&B each night, with its pleasant wallpaper, tasteful country scene prints, soft carpets, warm, clean bedding. He feared that he might open Vanessa's door to find himself looking at a version of his own barely furnished, soulless flat, and step back into a life he was subconsciously trying to leave behind.

It wasn't as bad as he had feared. She had furniture, a small television, even a mantelpiece with a scattering of family photos. But there was a carelessness about the place —unopened post, bent and crumpled beside the doormat, unwashed clothes left scattered, a flickering bulb when he turned on a hallway light—that put both Vanessa and himself into the same category of half-life, weighed down and held back by past trauma, unable to break free.

The letter was held against the fridge door with a magnet shaped like York Minster. Slim put the letter in his pocket, replaced the magnet and returned to his car before his thoughts could overcome him.

It took him a few minutes to compose himself before he opened the letter.

Dear Slim,

I'm not good with words. Never have been. I can't easily say what I want to say face to face with someone, because I'm concentrating on their reaction rather than my words, and that makes them come out garbled and cluttered.

Many years ago, while I was working at Oak House, I did a bad thing. I know it was a bad thing and I've lived with it ever since. I ruined someone's life and I think that all the things that have happened since have been as a result of that. I might not have gone to prison but I got what I deserved, and I think I'm not finished being punished yet.

What I felt for Jason ... wasn't just love. It was total obsession. I was fourteen when I first met him, and back then I was still starry-eyed and innocent. He took my breath away. I couldn't believe he would have any interest in me, and that he did made me feel like the most special person in the world. He was my first, and I rather naively dreamed that he would also be my last.

Except it didn't take long to realise there were others. In hindsight I can see him as the player that he was, but at the time I was completely taken in by his lies. Over the few weeks we were seeing each other, my obsession with him began to get darker.

He always insisted that when the time came, he would leave Maria and be with me. Often when I was around the circus people, pretending to be a fan or doing some stupid school project so I was there in case Jason wanted to sneak me into his caravan or behind a hedge somewhere, I would see her, stretching, practicing, training. She reminded me of a swan, all grace and beauty, and I began to hate her, because I knew I could never compete. I know now that she was only a handful of years older than I was, barely out of school, but in those days I looked on her as something magical, like a fairytale princess. I would always be in her shadow, no matter what he said.

And then, when he told me he was planning to leave, my thoughts took an even darker turn. He said their manager had been cheating them all, and that he wanted to teach him a lesson. He said he would come back for me when he could, but I took my own conclusions and assumed he would be leaving with her.

It was unexpected that I found myself working at Oak House those couple of weeks that September. After the residents were all in bed, I was free to do as I wished, and there was a fire door at the back which I could prop open a little so I could get back in without being seen. I crept out one night and went to see Jason at his caravan, only to see him and Maria together. It broke my heart, but I still couldn't see Jason for what he was. Instead, I began to regard her as some kind of

*she-devil standing in our way. If Maria was gone, Jason and me
could be together. At least that's what I thought.*

*A few nights later, I took a knife from the kitchen at Oak House and
sneaked out after dinner, while the residents were in the television
lounge. I knew there was a circus show in progress, but don't know
what I intended to do. I didn't have a plan. I went looking for Maria
but when I got into the backstage area, she had already gone up to her
harness.*

*I'd been around the performers a lot, and no one paid me any
attention. I found myself in the shadows below the scaffolding on
which Maria was standing. I didn't know what I was doing, but as I
stood there, my anger boiling over, I hacked at a couple of the nearest
ropes. I didn't plan to hurt her, not then. I just wanted to ruin her act,
make her look a fool, bring her down to my level.*

*I'm not sure to this day what I did, because it wasn't until more than
an hour later when I first heard the sirens of an ambulance. I was
pretending to sleep in the reception area and David appeared, scolding
me for being incompetent. He ordered me to get back to work. A few of
the residents were still downstairs, so I had to return them to their
rooms. There had been another temporary girl on that night who had
just gone home, and when I took Mrs. Bellingham upstairs, I found
she had put Mrs. Thompson into Mrs. Bellingham's room by mistake,
and the old woman had fallen asleep. No one liked Mrs. Thompson.
She couldn't speak due to a stroke or something, but she had a hollow
glare that made you feel detested. She had lumpy arthritic fingers, but
she would tap on the arms of her chair and make this wild, hideous
chuckle. I hated dealing with her and wasn't about to wake her up.
Mrs. Bellingham, however was lovely. She was suffering from
dementia but when she was all there she was a delightful lady. There
were no free rooms at the time, so I took her up to Mrs. Thompson's*

room and promised myself I would move her back to her own room in the morning before she got confused.

I thought nothing more of it until an hour later when I saw the clown. I didn't know what had happened over at the circus, but I know that clown had come for me. He was searching the house, looking for me. And when he couldn't find me, he took out his anger on two innocent old women.

Maria fell because of me. And those two women died because of me.

Everything was my fault.

I'm so sorry.

Vanessa

44

IT TOOK a while for Slim to bring himself to move after reading Vanessa's letter. For a long time he could do nothing other than stare out of the window at the grey streets outside, his thoughts filled with images of a life gone awry.

Another piece. But there was still more. Like a wounded bloodhound dragging itself forward, unable even in its dying moments to give up the trail, Slim forced himself to turn the ignition, to pull out from the pavement, and to head onwards to the next lead.

He drove to Stourbridge, to Kevin Dean's house.

Kevin wasn't home, so Slim waited in the car until a man with a vague resemblance to Derek walked past him, bag slung over his shoulder, and turned into Kevin's gate. Slim was out of the car in a moment, his feet moving as though he were floating on air. He had covered the distance to the gate in the time it had taken Kevin to pull his keyring from his pocket, and as he slid the key into the lock, Slim came up behind him, shoving him forwards as the door opened. Kevin let out a shocked gasp as he fell,

Slim falling clumsily on top of him, kicking the door closed behind them. Even though Kevin had a couple of inches on Slim in height, Slim had the advantage. He readied himself for a fight, only for Kevin to cry out, 'Gav! Gav! I'm sorry, man! I didn't say anything!'

Slim pushed himself away and sat up as Kevin crawled forward. He got a hand on a glass panelled door and pulled it open, revealing a small kitchen beyond. A little terrier came scampering through, licked Kevin's hand, then looked at Slim and gave a gruff, angry bark.

'I'm not Gavin,' Slim said, pulling himself up as Kevin, turning around, realised his mistake. 'But I'd be interested to know why you thought I might be. I'm sorry, Kevin, but I really needed to speak to you.'

'You're that detective guy, aren't you? You can't just barge in here. I could call the police—'

'Yes, you could, and you have a perfect right to. Please though, just answer a couple of questions and then I'll leave.'

As Kevin stood up, Slim's cheeks burned with shame. Kevin looked like his whole life had flashed before his eyes. His lip trembled, and he looked about to cry.

'You can't let him find out,' he said, voice hollow, wavering. 'You don't mess with Gav Thomas. Not then, not now.'

'Jason Felton. You took him up to the Cloverdale Hills the night the Southern Cross Circus closed down for good.'

'Gav said he'd been sniffing around Elaine. Said he needed to teach him a lesson.'

'I heard they were mates.'

'Yeah, I suppose. Not close, though. Not close enough that Gav wouldn't have smacked him up if he played around with Elaine.'

'Gav said you roughed him up before you took him up to the hill. How bad?'

Kevin shrugged. 'We shoved him around a bit. Scared him. A couple of guys might have got a punch in, but he was Gav's, you know?'

'So Jason was coherent?'

'Yeah, totally. Whined like a girl the whole way up. We had to keep the doors locked in case he made a run for it.'

'I've seen pictures of Jason. He was big, strong, a gymnast.'

Kevin shook his head. 'Ah, man. You didn't know Gav. Back then, he was nails. Rest of us couldn't get out of there fast enough. We thought Jason was gonna die.'

'And you didn't see Jason or Gavin again that night?'

Kevin shook his head again. 'Gav went away for a while. Don't know where. Laid low I suppose. Next I heard from him was months later, he'd been given five years for holding up a petrol station with a kitchen knife. Jason, we heard nothing. Kept waiting for a body to show up.' He rubbed his face, his eyes haunted by his memories. 'I couldn't walk up there for years. I knew Gav must have hidden him up there somewhere.' He let out a long sigh. 'What was left of him.'

45

Slim left his car in a supermarket car park and wandered the streets of Stourbridge, letting his thoughts tumble and churn, throwing everything he had learned into the mix and hoping an answer came out. More than once he found himself at the door to a pub, clawing himself away, inches from falling back into his old trap. He didn't need it, he screamed at himself. He could do this without the crutch.

It was dark when he found his way back to the car, cold and exhausted, his mind aching. He switched on his car light and took out the folder of photographs, some from Derek, some he had taken himself. He looked at the notes he had made on the travel documents, on Kay's handwriting analysis, on the letter sent to Maria. He looked at the pictures he had of Jason and Lowery Powell. He looked at the documents he had got from the council. He had a theory, and could connect almost all of the dots, but there was one corner of the puzzle that still eluded him.

The two old women. Who had killed them, and why.

Sure, Robert might have had a beef with his brother, but enough to commit murder?

Don had sent him the coroner's reports. Both deaths had been listed as natural causes—possibly due to pressure asserted by David Bellingham, in the same way he had pressured Vanessa to keep her mouth shut, but there was evidence in the details. Both, for example, had recorded bruising on the inside of the lips, a sign of compression. Slim was in no doubt they had been murdered, but by whom? And why?

It was nearly eleven o'clock when he returned to Meadow Cross, desperate for a few hours' sleep, but as he approached the B&B from the north, a flashing light up ahead caught his eye. He pulled in to the side of the road, got out and walked a little further ahead until his worst fears were confirmed: there was a police car parked outside the B&B.

Kevin Dean must have called the police, and had he passed them Jessica's number it would have been easy to find out where Slim was staying. He went back to the car, turned around, and headed back towards Hagley, before having a change of mind and making a right turn and heading for the Cloverdale Hills.

It crossed his mind to just keep driving, but what would be the point? He had given Jane his current address. He couldn't hide, but neither could he explain himself. At best he would get moved on, at worst taken into custody.

He was still driving, wondering what to do, when his phone, propped in the cup holder in front of the gearbox, buzzed with an incoming call. He glanced at the display, fearing the police, but saw Donald Lane's number. Aware he was already in trouble, he put the phone to his ear with his left hand, controlling the car with his right.

'Don? It's late. Are you all right?'

'Yeah, Slim, I just didn't hear back so I was wondering what you thought of that email I sent you?'

Slim rubbed his eyes. 'Jason's reports. I read it. It was interesting. It gave me a few things to think about.'

'Not that one,' Don said. 'The other one. The one about the foster mother drowning the young girl in the bath.'

A chill ran down Slim's back. 'No, I hadn't got to that one,' he said, the words empty and echoing. 'I … haven't read that one yet.'

'Well, you'd better find somewhere where you can. It could explain a few things.'

46

AT NEARLY MIDNIGHT Slim didn't have a lot of options. He had his laptop, but without an internet connection he couldn't view his emails. He drove around, looking for somewhere he could get a Wi-Fi signal, but there wasn't much open so late, and the nearest motorway service area had just closed when he pulled up. In the end, he found himself in Stourbridge, outside the closed library, shining a torch through the window in an attempt to read the Wi-Fi password on a poster on the wall. Luckily it was a memorable phrase rather than a forgettable list of numbers and letters, but even with the Wi-Fi connected to his laptop as he crouched in an alcove by the door, the signal was so weak it took an age for his browser to load.

A couple of times, sirens rose in the distance, and Slim wondered if they might be tracking him, if the police were right now heading for the library. He had gone too far with Kevin and he knew it, and with his record it was likely he would do more custodial time.

At long last his browser loaded, and he opened the email from Don, quickly downloading the attachments and copying the contents of the message, before hurrying back to his car.

It was long after midnight but he needed coffee. Aware he was leaving a trail but beyond caring, he bought coffee and some snack food from a 24-hour garage, then drove back out into the countryside, finally turning down a secluded farm lane before he switched off the headlights and pulled out his computer.

Slim, I also found this. I did an extensive search using some of the names you've given me over the last couple of weeks, and they led me to this. I don't know how significant it is, but it must be, right? Let me know what you think.

Don

The first attachment was a newspaper report from 1978.

Foster mother convicted of manslaughter

"Loving mother" sentenced to 12 years for accidental drowning of foster daughter

A jury at Birmingham Crown Court today convicted Charlotte Haddon (67) from the Stockford area of manslaughter in the case of the June, 1976 drowning of a seven-year-old girl now named by the courts as Stephanie Louise Gavin. Based on evidence presented to the court, Mrs. Haddon, well-known and active in her local community, a jury decided in a 10-2 majority that Mrs. Haddon should be convicted of manslaughter, although she was acquitted of the more serious charge of second-degree murder. Mr. Justice Williams based his sentencing on testimonies made by older children formerly held in her care (names withheld for legal reasons), and made it clear that should she be released earlier than her sentence decreed, she should never be allowed to work in social or childcare again. Five other children in her care at the time of the crime were placed in alternative homes.

Slim could hardly breathe as he opened the second attachment, another local news article, this one from a tabloid.

"Monster Mother" to be released on humanitarian grounds
Due to the declining mental state of Charlotte Haddon, convicted in 1978 of the manslaughter of a girl in her foster care, it has been announced that she will be released early from her sentence. Despite public uproar at the decision, mostly in light of the testimonies of children formerly held in her care that have emerged in recent years depicting life in the Haddon household as "Satanic" and "horrific beyond words", the judge in the case said that his decision is based on the fact that Mrs. Haddon is no longer of any danger to society. She is to be given a new identity and moved to an undisclosed address, thought to be a residential care home.

The third attachment was a photograph. It appeared to have been cut or clipped from a book or newspaper, and at the outset was a family portrait. A large, jovial man stood with his hand on the shoulder of a seated thin-faced woman, unsmiling, hands clasped neatly on her lap. Around them stood six children: two older boys, a teenage girl, and three much younger children: a boy of around eight, a girl perhaps a year younger, then a little boy, perhaps five.

Beneath was a caption: *The Haddon family in happier days. (Clockwise from left) Jake, Lewis, Charlotte, Paul, Tiffany, Thomas, Stephanie, Jason.*

Slim stared at the picture for a long time. There were stories in the eyes of the children that might take a long time to unpick, and he hoped those who could had found peace in their adult lives.

The youngest three were his concern, though. There was a similarity in their faces that suggested they were siblings. The girl, Stephanie Gavin, was surely the one who had died, and Jason, the littlest, was a cherubic fallacy of the man he would become.

And then there was the third.

Thomas.

And if he shared the same surname name as his sister, his name was Thomas Gavin.

The man Slim knew now as Gavin Thomas.

As adults, Jason and Thomas had only a passing resemblance, the paths of their lives diverging, society taking its toll. As children, though, they shared the same facial structure, the same look in their eyes.

Slim closed his laptop. Aware of what he had to do, he put the car into reverse and drove swiftly out of the farm lane, turned around, and headed for Meadow Cross.

47

He hadn't expected his old lockpick to work on a church door, but it had, the heavy, clunky bolt rattling as it turned. Inside, the church had been warmer than he had expected, but he had still appreciated the blanket he had brought from the back of his car as he assembled a pile of kneelers into a rough mattress, then lay down between the first and second rows of pews. Caffeine loaded and wired with the thrill of the chase, he hadn't expected to get any sleep but surprisingly he had, awaking some hours later to the sound of the opening door, to find light streaming down on him through the high stained-glass windows.

Groggy from sleep but immediately composing himself with an old Armed Forces level of precision, he was sitting up on the front row of pews by the time he heard Gavin Thomas enter the knave, heavy footfalls echoing on the flagstones.

Slim stared straight ahead, thinking of the envelope he had placed outside Katie Julius's door in the middle of the night. It contained his most important documents, plus his notes and theories. "If I don't return for this by tonight, please pass to the police" he had written on the outside.

He hoped he would be able to hand over the documents himself, but first he needed to give Gavin a chance to explain … and maybe to fill in a few holes that were still missing.

The footsteps had stopped. Slim waited. It felt like an age before Gavin said, 'What are you doing here?'

'We need to talk,' Slim said. Slowly he stood up and turned around. Gavin was standing by the pulpit, wearing a long, unfastened jacket over jeans and a sweater, holding an assortment of leaflets.

'I've told you everything.'

Slim shook his head. 'No, you haven't. But you're going to now. Because if you don't, I'll tell what I know to the police and let them decide.'

Gavin stared for a moment, then took a few steps forward. Slim saw how his free hand was bunched into a fist, and sighed. He didn't want it to be this way, but it would be, if he had no choice.

'I know what happened to your sister. I'm so very sorry.'

The tension left Gavin's body and he sagged, reaching for the back of a nearby pew for support.

'I can understand why you wanted revenge, and when you saw the opportunity, you took it. I think I would have done the same thing in your situation. However, an innocent woman also died.'

Gavin's face crumpled. 'How was I to know they'd put the old bitch in the wrong room—'

'You realised after you'd smothered Margaret Bellingham that it wasn't Carrie after all. Or, as you knew her, Charlotte.'

'I waited until it was done until I turned on the light,'

Gavin said. 'I was afraid if I saw her—or worse, she saw me—that I wouldn't have what it took to go through with it. I wanted to see her dead though. I so desperately wanted to see her dead. But it wasn't … it wasn't her.'

'So you went looking for her?'

'I tried a few doors. Not all of them were labeled. In the end though … I found her. And then….'

Slim walked over to Gavin and sat down nearby. Gavin stared at Slim for a moment then sat down across the aisle.

'You have a business, you have a job,' Slim said. 'You're unattached, from what I can see. You have the means. I can give you three days to get away. Go anywhere. Anywhere you want. That's the best I can do for you, Gavin. But please, first tell me what happened.'

Gavin scoffed. 'You're the detective. Why don't you tell me?'

Slim nodded. 'That's fair enough. You kept in touch with Jason, or maybe your respective foster homes did that for you?'

'We were split up,' Gavin said with a bitter snarl. 'They thought I was a bad influence on him. What did they expect after what happened? I got churned through the system, he got lucky in the end. Luckier than me, at any rate. We were allowed contact, but not face to face until he left school.'

'When he began working for Southern Cross, you got close again?'

'It was like we were never separated.'

'Yet Stephanie's death haunted you both.'

'Jason had blocked most of it out, he was too young.'

'That's why it was you that went into the house?'

'Yes. She used to taunt me, tell me how she'd held Stephanie under. She used to tap on the side of my bed, tell me that was how Stephanie's feet had sounded as they kicked against the side of the bath. Told me I'd be next if I didn't behave, no one would believe me if I told. So I said nothing. It was one of the older kids who shopped her in the end, and then everything started to come out.'

'You found out she had been released and sent to Oak House how exactly?'

'Earlier that year they had an outing for all the residents and wheeled them over to Southern Cross for a private performance. I was working the door. I couldn't believe it was her at first, but Jason recognised her too, and we couldn't both be wrong. It was a cruel, cruel coincidence.' Gavin clenched his fists together and punched the back of the pews in front hard enough to cause the wood to make a sharp cracking sound. 'David Bellingham would do anything for money.'

'She didn't recognise you?'

'She was barely alive. It should have been enough to see her like that, but it wasn't. I wanted her dead. I wanted it like I've never wanted anything else in my life.'

'So you planned it? Am I right that Maria's fall was a coincidence?'

Gavin nodded. 'We planned it for that night because it was the last of the season. We could both take off and few questions would be asked. No one, except perhaps David Bellingham, knew Charlotte's true identity, and he wouldn't risk the damage to his reputation and business by letting it slip. There was no connection to us.'

'Jason was a player, so you had a motive for taking him up to the Cloverdale Hills. You were both going to vanish after that, but you came back. Did you hide a scooter up there or something?'

'Bicycles. It was all downhill. A five-minute ride.'

Slim nodded. 'Simple. And you were to go into the house while Jason kept watch?'

'We threw on some overalls and cheap clown masks in case we were seen. Ordinarily we'd have stood out, but not with a circus right there. No one would have looked twice.'

'How did you get into the house?'

Gavin chuckled. 'Even by then I knew how to break in. I was going to go through a downstairs window, but I noticed a fire door slightly ajar. It was a heavy thing and someone had pulled it shut but not closed it properly.'

'Jason wasn't involved in the murder. What was he planning to do?'

'Lowery Powell was set to make a seasonal closing speech. While he was occupied, Jason was going to clean out his caravan, take whatever he could find. None of the performers were properly paid. There was a lot of bad feeling about it. He wanted to screw Powell however he could.'

'Only while Jason was there, Powell showed up, didn't he? Perhaps he wanted to hide out after Maria's fall, or perhaps make some getaway plans of his own.'

Gavin looked down, then gave a slow nod. 'I don't know what happened,' he said. 'He was dead when I got there. Jason and me, we did what we had to do, then we got out of there.'

'You flew to Malaga, didn't you? Jason used Lowery's passport.'

'We were desperate, and stupid. It was Jason's idea. He'd found Powell's passport while ransacking the caravan, before Powell showed up. At first we were just going to bin it somewhere, make it look like Powell had jumped the country. It was Jason's idea to actually use it.' He shook his head, then gave a dry chuckle. 'We should have been stopped, but it was a budget airline, and they were busy. Jason wore some hat he bought in a souvenir shop inside the airport and then strolled through as though he owned the place. It was enough. Once in Spain, we laid low awhile, then went our separate ways. I didn't want Lowery's money, so Jason took it. Eventually I came home, and ended up in more trouble. The police came knocking regularly, but for that, however, they never came.' He sighed again and ran a hand through what was left of his hair. 'Until now.'

'I'm not the police.'

'But that's your next step, isn't it? You wanted blood, and you got it.'

'I told you. Three days.'

Gavin scoffed. 'What gives you the right to start making decisions on justice?'

Slim held his gaze. 'I was dealt a poor hand in life,' he said. 'But it was still better than some. Better than yours. I can't walk away from this, because there are too many people involved who deserve answers. But I can give you a start.'

Gavin's hand slid inside his jacket, and a claw hammer appeared in his fingers. He turned it over in his hands, then looked up at Slim, who hadn't even flinched.

'Is that the same one you used on Charlotte's grave?'

Gavin looked surprised. 'Huh. No, but … you noticed.'

'Someone didn't like her, that was obvious.'

Gavin looked down at the hammer. 'Could you stop me?' he asked.

'That's quite a tool for a man of the cloth,' Slim said.

'Charlotte wasn't a mistake, but I made others. And some people have long memories.' Gavin looked up, meeting Slim's eyes. 'Could you stop me?' he said again.

'I've covered my back,' Slim said. 'I learned to the hard way. Take what I'm offering, Gavin. You've done enough time for your crimes. You don't need to do more.'

Gavin turned the hammer over again. It disappeared back into an inner pocket of his jacket, and he stood up.

'I won't thank you,' he said. 'You've destroyed everything I know.'

Slim didn't look up. 'What is it they say? Tomorrow is a new day. I hope the weather's good for you, Gavin. I mean that.'

For a few seconds Gavin stood over him, his breathing hoarse, almost desperate, and Slim wondered if this was the sound Vanessa had heard while crouched in the store room at Oak House. The sound of a man who, in attempting to right a wrong, had at the same time made a terrible mistake. Then Gavin turned and walked away. Slim listened to his footsteps as they receded, then the thud of the church door as it closed.

It was a long time before he could bring himself to move. In the end, he had no choice. He still had things to do.

48

THE ENVELOPE SLIM had left for Katie was still where he had left it, resting outside her door. He retrieved it without bothering her, returned to his car, and drove out of town.

For the next three days, he drove around the area, sleeping in his car down quiet country lanes, tucked into the back corners of public car parks, staying out of the way, keeping his head down, his phone switched off.

When it came time to break his silence, he first called an old colleague, one with whom there was no love lost, but a mutual respect and even an element of trust. Ben Holland had served for a time as Slim's squad leader during his Armed Forces days, and had gone on to gain a position of authority within the Metropolitan Police.

'Ben? It's me, Slim.'

'It's been a long time, Slim.'

Slim smiled. The coldness was there, as always. Something would be wrong otherwise.

'I'm good,' Slim said, answering the unasked question. 'And you?'

'Been better but I'll live. To what do I owe the pleasure of this call?'

'I have a lead for you.'

'Oh?'

As always, there had been a few questions left unasked, some answers he might never know for sure. Slim had let Gavin go with the biggest of them still hanging in the air, but felt certain he knew the answer.

The construction work had begun on Robert Bellingham's extension in August of 1992, according to the planning permission document Slim had obtained from the local council. And from the pictures he had seen, by the day of the circus's final performance, the basement had been excavated, and the retaining walls erected. The ground around the walls was yet to be filled in, and piles of earth and rocks had stood nearby, waiting to be replaced.

Less than fifty yards away had been the nearest of the circus caravans.

Slim doubted the builders would have looked twice when they used their JCBs to fill in the remainder of the debris when next they came to work, but if they had they might have seen protruding parts of a human body, lying hastily buried in the space behind the nearest retaining wall. Also, for police investigating Maria's fall, it would have been an easy find.

Had they been looking.

Upon searching the circus master's caravan, however, they would have found his passport missing, the safe and that night's cash boxes empty, and begun a search of a different kind. By the end of the following day, however, Lowery Powell would have been buried.

'I know the location of a body. You'll need a permit and the resources to do an excavation.'

'How sure are you?'

'I'm certain.'

While he wasn't one hundred percent, he definitely had enough background to argue his case. Coaker's recording device had chosen its moment to work while left in Slim's coat pocket, and the conversation with Gavin Thomas was safely stored on a computer hard drive. He intended to keep his promise to Gavin, but it was there if he needed it.

There was a pause. Then Ben said, 'All right. Give me what details you have and I'll see what I can do.'

'Thanks. I appreciate it, Ben.'

'Sure, Slim.'

Ben Holland hung up, and Slim gave a tired sigh. There were other loose ends he was slowly clearing up. Don had managed to dig up Gavin Thomas's N.I. payments record, which revealed he had briefly worked part time at the Stourbridge Public Library, as part of a prisoner rehabilitation scheme. Perhaps he had thought that removing the microfiche pages of an old newspaper would help cover evidence of a crime.

He was yet to figure out why Robert Bellingham had been committing disability fraud for the past thirty years. Watching his brother work while spending his own time lounging about might have been some form of revenge. Slim had drafted a letter to Social Services, but changed his mind and decided not to send it; when a body was discovered on his property, that would be scandal enough.

Neither also, did he have much sympathy for David, a man both willing to take government money to home a child killer as well as to cover up evidence of his mother's murder in order to protect his business. Perhaps the exposure of both and their connotations might have an effect on Oak House's short-term business, but it would survive. David might have to drop his prices for a while, but there would always be customers.

Later that day, he went to a local police station and handed himself in, at the same time explaining his investigation and passing to the police what he was willing to share. To his surprise, Kevin Dean, perhaps not wanting the trouble, had already dropped his complaint, and Slim found himself free to go.

He headed back to Meadow Cross, where first he stopped in to pay his account with Jane, then walked up to Katie Julius's house, where he thanked her for her help over a cup of coffee. This time she got out the good stuff.

Afterwards, he went to the Spar where he found Derek behind the counter. He returned the photographs, then apologised for the VHS tape. He explained how he had bought an old player, and the tape had got damaged.

'It's all right,' Derek said. 'Mum never looks at them. She probably won't notice.'

'How is your mum?'

Derek shrugged. 'She's been a bit down,' he said. 'She had a thing for the Reverend, but it seems he's left town. The pub he owned has closed and everything.'

'That's too bad, but she's a pretty lady, your mum. She'll find someone else.'

'What about you?' Derek asked, the note of hope in his voice making Slim smile. 'Are you sticking around?'

'I'm afraid not,' Slim said. 'It's time to move on. Good luck with Helen.'

'Thanks for your advice.'

'No problem. Take care, Derek.'

He had lied about the VHS tape. A couple of hours later, he took it into a patch of woodland, doused it with some paraffin, then set it alight. When nothing was left but a few charred remains, he scooped them up, then dropped them into a stream he crossed on the walk back to his car.

He wanted the narrative, when it came out, to head in

a certain direction. Jason, in his absence, could absorb the blame. Vanessa had suffered enough, and from what Slim could tell, there was no other evidence that could prove she was in the performer's area on the night of Maria's accident.

He had already spoken to Maria, however, and after disposing of the tape, he drove to Birmingham New Street Station, where he was just in time to pick her up off the train.

'Will it make any difference?' she asked him, as they drove through the city centre. 'I mean, it's been so long. What can possibly be done to change things now? You somehow managed to dig all this up, upend people's lives after thirty years, and you think I have the power to make anything better? I always wondered what happened, but I've moved on. I dealt with it and got on with my life.'

'You did,' Slim said. 'But not everyone did. Some people have carried the events of that night with them ever since.'

'And how can I change that?'

'You be surprised what you can do with words,' Slim said.

When they arrived at the hospital, Slim found Vanessa sitting up in bed, reading a magazine propped up on a stand beside her. She looked better, but still frail. A tube still protruded from her arm.

'I have someone with me,' Slim said. 'Someone important I'd like you to meet.'

He called Maria into the room. At first Vanessa frowned, shaking her head, then she gave a little gasp and covered her mouth with her hands. A tear beaded and rolled down her cheek.

'Maria,' she whispered, sobbing now.

Maria sat down on a chair beside Vanessa's bed and took Vanessa's hands in hers.

'Vanessa,' she said.

'I'm sorry. I'm so sorry.'

'I know. And I forgive you, Vanessa. We were both taken in, we were both fooled. And I think we've both suffered enough, don't you?'

Slim watched the two women, both crying now as Maria leaned forward and pulled Vanessa into a powerful hug. He watched them, his heart breaking, mending, then perhaps breaking again, then he slowly backed out of the room, went down the corridor, and got himself a coffee out of a machine in the lobby.

Both had been blinded by the circus lights, and both, in their way, had fallen. But perhaps, if some good could come from all of it, perhaps they could both begin to heal and move forward.

He sighed, wincing at the weak taste of the coffee, then sat down on a plastic chair, leaned his head back against the wall, and closed his eyes.

END

ABOUT THE AUTHOR

Jack Benton is a pen name of Chris Ward, the author of the dystopian *Tube Riders* series, the horror/science fiction *Tales of Crow* series, and the *Endinfinium* YA fantasy series, as well as numerous other well-received stand alone novels.

The Circus Lights is the eighth mystery to feature John "Slim" Hardy. There will be more…

Chris would love to hear from you:
www.amillionmilesfromanywhere.net/tokyolost
chrisward@amillionmilesfromanywhere.net

ACKNOWLEDGMENTS

Many thanks as always go to those who helped with this book. Jenny Avery for her incredible knowledge and eye for detail, Elizabeth Mackey for the cover, and Paige Sayer for proofreading. And as always, to two of my earliest champions, Jenny Twist and John Dalton.

Finally, for those of you who support me via Patreon, thanks very much. In no special order: Mike Wright, Carl Rod, Rosemary Kenny, Jane Ornelas, Ron, Gail Beth Le Vine, Anja Peerdeman, Sharon Kenneson, Jennie Brown, Leigh McEwan, Amaranth Dawe, Janet Hodgson, Katherine Crispin, Mike Wright, and Gibbo the Great.

And for everyone who's Bought me a Coffee recently: Cesar Sandoval, Ann Chesterton, Nova Kay, Someone, Jennie B, Mary, Richard Herndon, Claire, Ian Yates-Laughton, Jim Naughton, Rowan Anderson, Andrea Richards, Malcolm from Canada, Elizabeth M. Dykes, Rachel G, Keith Turner, Sheri Bellefeuille, Niall Nicolson, Amelie Eva, Paul M, Laurie Jones, Aileen MacKinnon, Att, Irena, Michael Fidler, Lindsay G Cowan, Spyke, Rosemary, Marianne, Denise Nicholson, Someone, Janet, and Christine Henderson. Thank you. Your support means so much.

Last and not least, to all my readers. Thank you for supporting my books and I look forward to bringing you the next John "Slim" Hardy adventure.

JB

April 2023

Printed in Great Britain
by Amazon

39704810R00121